The Scorpion's Helper

Susan W. McMichaels

Lucky Bat Books

ALSO BY SUSAN W. MCMICHAELS

Journey out of the Garden:
St. Francis of Assisi and the Process of Individuation

A Lucky Bat Book

The Scorpion's Helper

Cover Design by Guilherme Gustavo Condeixa

10-9-8-7-6-5-4-3-2-1
ISBN: 978-1-939051-83-7

The detail from Giotto's Annunciation to St. Anne on the front cover is in the public domain and is available at: http://commons.wikimedia.org/wiki/File:Giotto_di_Bondone_-_No._3_Scenes_from_the_Life_of_Joachim_-_3._Annunciation_to_St_Anne_-_WGA09171.jpg.

Also available in digital formats

Published by Lucky Bat Books
LuckyBatBooks.com

JERUSALEM, B.C.E.

THE CHILD WAS sitting in a street that led to the marketplace, her scabby knees pulled up to her chest. The rags she wore barely covered her enough for decency, not nearly enough for protection against the wind and rain that ushered in the bleak months of winter.

The woman who pressed a small silver coin into the child's outstretched hand saw eyes dulled by hunger and an appalling loneliness, disturbing in a girl who could not yet be ten.

The woman imagined the mute child trapped in a world of utter silence, damaged from birth or by some accident, never guessing that her hearing was as acute as that of some nocturnal animal.

For the next several weeks the woman set aside a small coin for the child from the money her husband placed on the table each market day. Finally, after many nights of worry and restless dreams, she led the child home.

CHAPTER 1

Jerusalem

On the first day the child thought, I am warm. I am dry. I do not hunger. I do not thirst. I am not kicked or spat upon.

Each night she woke from her nightmare. *My father hurts me while Mother sleeps.* The nightmare was a memory as real as the blanket that couldn't keep her from shivering in fear.

Gradually her attention became more particular. *This room is dark when I sleep. It brightens when the woman wakes, and then there is food. The woman goes behind the curtain with the man when the room grows dark. The man does not hurt her. She does not cry or scream in fear. Within these walls is safety. I may watch and listen from the place of refuge that has found me.*

The girl ate from a bowl the warm red color of the clay that formed it. A crack zigzagged like a bolt of lightning from the rim of the bowl to its base. She often ran her finger along the crack and remembered the day the woman handed the bowl to her, saying to the man that it would do for their little servant's meals.

In addition to the bowl, the woman had given her a name. The man laughed when Anne said they would call the child Ozeret. "She's deaf and mute," Joachim said. "Why does she need a name?"

"It is our duty to name her," Anne had answered. "I give her the name that means Helper because that is what she will be."

Ozeret learned to chop vegetables and cook lentils and bake bread for the evening meal. As she scoured the table and rubbed it with oil, she noticed how the wide planks joined together to make a surface both useful and beautiful and how that surface gleamed when she had finished polishing it. She scrubbed the dishes and goblets and saw that they were smoother and more brightly glazed than the earthenware water jug by the door.

At night Ozeret listened to the sounds, as clear and distinct as raindrops breaking the surface of a puddle, Anne spoke to Joachim behind the curtain of the bedroom.

At first the words bore no relation to each other. But slowly, in the same way Ozeret came to name the taste and texture of what she ate, she began to connect the words into story that fed an imagination as starved, or more, than her body had been.

One night Ozeret listened through the bedroom curtain to Anne's story of the first two people who ever lived in the world. Ozeret imagined the first man and woman in the tiny walled garden behind this house, with its fig tree and its bench. She saw a beautiful woman, her mistress when she was young, pluck a ripe fig from the tree and offer it to the man.

Ozeret puzzled over the way the story ended. Why were the man and woman punished for eating the fruit and banished from the garden? Why didn't the owner of the garden protect the forbidden tree? Her mistress was so much wiser than the god who ruled the garden. Anne locked up what was precious to keep it safe.

At first Ozeret tested the cupboard door that hid her mistress's herbs and spices and was relieved to find it safely locked. She pressed her nose against the smooth olive wood and breathed deeply to remember the smells that snaked seductively into the room each time her mistress unlocked the cupboard and opened the door.

As Ozeret took on more responsibility for grinding herbs and spices, she came to understand that air and light would destroy the miracle of the seasonings locked in the cupboard. She became as jealous of the contents of the cupboard as her mistress. There was no longer need for lock and key to prevent her from opening the door.

Why, Ozeret wondered, didn't the god of the first people teach his children as wisely as her mistress taught her, an abandoned beggar?

Through the bedroom curtain Ozeret heard Joachim tell Anne that the god who created the first people expected them to do what was right and fitting according to his laws. They could prove their worthiness to be his chosen people by doing whatever he asked of them and trusting him without question.

Ozeret could feel the rage in Anne's reply.

"A god who tempts his creatures beyond their capacity to understand, or their ability to choose, is like a parent who puts a jug of precious oil on the floor next to a babe just learning to crawl," Ozeret heard her mistress hiss. "You speak, Husband, as if words have no connection to this world and its ways and the ways of its people. Don't talk to me in the words of your god and his priests."

Then there was silence followed by the gentle voice of the man. Ozeret rose from her pallet and tiptoed across the cold stones of the floor to better hear his words.

"I must go to the Temple, my Beloved," he said, "and follow the rules of the god of our people. You change the stories of our people and our god until I lose my way. I must study the words on the scrolls and perform the rituals and sacrifices as a man and a priest until a messiah frees us from oppression and brings us to power as the greatest people on earth."

Ozeret heard her mistress respond, in a voice choked by her tears, "My messiah will see the world as the upside down place it is, where power goes to those who are evil, and the meek, like our faithful Ozeret, suffer for sins they did not commit."

Ozeret was startled by the sound of her name. She moved as quietly as she could back to her pallet and fell into a restless sleep.

Later Ozeret woke to the sound of her mistress weeping. Her own face felt wet. She remembered. *Mother slapped my face and told me to be still.*

Ozeret crept back to the bedroom curtain and listened as Anne's weeping turned again to words. Anne told Joachim about Eve's hunger in the garden, a hunger for knowledge and understanding more powerful than blind obedience. Anne spoke the thoughts in the mind of Lot's wife, her need to witness the horror that had befallen her city, before she was turned into a pillar of salt. Anne told of the terrible drowning of babies and children and creatures innocent of wrongdoing in the great flood of the wrath of Joachim's god. She described the beauty of the rainbow and how quickly it faded, disappearing as completely and returning as unpredictably as the mercy of the god of this world.

Ozeret, crouching by the curtain, remembered. *Father led me through the hills, in darkness and silence, and abandoned me in the city of Jerusalem.*

Ozeret listened as Anne imagined a different god, one who would enter the world of his creatures and share with them the anguish of their lives.

Then Anne wept with tears as raw and wild as an inconsolable child's. She wept for herself and for Joachim and for the deaf mute creature, Ozeret, in the next room. She wept for all the misery and disappointment and pain that seemed to darken the walls of Jerusalem even under the springtime sun.

Silently, hidden by the curtain, Ozeret wept too.

CHAPTER 2

Jerusalem, five years later

Ozeret opened her eyes. She felt the straw pallet beneath her. A coarse woolen blanket cocooned her body, all ribs and elbows and knees despite the food she was allowed each day.

Ozeret's stomach rumbled insistently, but the early discipline of starvation made her focus her mind elsewhere. She waited for the weeping to end and her mistress to rise from her bed and prepare for the day. Her mistress always wept when her husband was sent on some insulting errand by the chief priest of the Temple.

Ozeret could see that her master had grown too old to climb into the hills above the city and bargain with a shepherd for a sacrificial lamb. She wished she could perform the task for him.

Her mistress was old now too. Grief and shame lined her face and bowed her shoulders. She was childless. Her husband had fathered no children to people the House of David. There was no place of honor for her or for her husband among the priests and respectable Jewish families in Jerusalem.

Ozeret attended carefully to the pinging of the chamber pot beyond the curtain and the rustle of a night garment coming off and a daytime garment replacing it. She listened to her mistress gather her hair beneath the linen headscarf that concealed it from the gaze of anyone but her husband.

Ozeret wondered what her mistress's hair looked like. Her own, always clean and combed free of tangles and lice, was dark and fine and very straight. At night, Ozeret rubbed its softness against her cheek. But now, with her mistress about to enter the brightening room, Ozeret twisted her hair into a single braid and covered it with her own coarse scarf.

Ozeret went into the alley to do her business. The patch of sky above her was turning blue, and the spring morning was beginning to warm.

When she returned to the house, silence filled the room and an eerie light seeped under the bedroom curtain. Ozeret watched the bedroom curtain billow as if moved by a strong wind.

Suddenly her mistress cried out. Ozeret froze. Why did her mistress make the sound of nighttime love?

Soon the room filled with familiar morning light. The bedroom curtain settled in its usual folds. Ozeret moved away from the door and her body moved automatically into the preparation of her mistress's meal.

OZERET STOOD OUTSIDE the gates of the city watching Anne stare east towards the Mount of Olives. She was so hungry that she felt faint. Her mistress had rushed out of the house without eating the meal Ozeret prepared, and Ozeret had rushed after her.

A group of women clustered inside the gates. Ozeret shrank inside her black cloak, hoping her mistress was too absorbed in her own thoughts to hear the snatches of cruelty that drifted towards them through the gentle spring air.

"Still waiting for her ram to mount her," Ozeret heard a woman laugh coarsely.

Ozeret turned to glare at the woman inside the gate, forgetting for a moment that she was a deaf, mute servant girl. The woman felt the force of Ozeret's eyes, and her laugh turned into a cough. Silence fell over the women, and into the silence sang Anne's joyful cry, "He comes!"

Ozeret turned from the women inside the gate and moved closer to her mistress. She made out the figure of Joachim winding his way down the hillside through the flowering olive trees. Behind him was a shepherd. Ozeret could hear the lamb on the shepherd's shoulders bleating as pitifully and monotonously as a hungry infant.

Ozeret heard the shepherd cry out in pain and surprise. She turned to him and watched as he knelt down to look at his foot. The lamb stopped crying and seemed to be looking too.

Ozeret could hear her master and mistress whispering together, oblivious to the shepherd and the lamb, but she didn't attend to their words. All her attention was fixed on the scorpion stinging the shepherd's heel.

Ozeret walked over to the shepherd and took the staff lying in the dust beside him. She used the end of the staff to pry the scorpion from the shepherd's heel and then crushed the scorpion with her sandal. The shepherd stood up and settled the lamb on Ozeret's shoulders. Then he took his staff from her and limped his way back up the winding path.

Ozeret turned back to the gate. She listened intently as her mistress, twisting a strand of Joachim's gray hair around her finger, whispered into his ear, "We are to have our child at last."

OZERET SAT ON her pallet spinning wool into thread for a new tunic for her master. Her long fingers moved nimbly, accustomed to the task.

The very air in the room felt different since her mistress told her husband that their long-awaited child was to be born. Even the dust motes seemed to dance in the spring sunlight that streamed through the open window, and the sound of babies crying and children playing in the street made her mistress laugh with joy.

Each day brought women smiling their congratulations. Each night the master returned from the Temple with his head held high. Ozeret watched and listened.

Ozeret remembered the long-ago time when her mistress told her master, "Look at our little servant. She's filling out nicely. She's quite pretty now that she has some meat on her bones. And Joachim, there's intelligence within her. She learns so quickly."

Listening with delight, Ozeret had redoubled her efforts to pound the spices for the wine exactly as her mistress had taught her.

But now that her mistress's belly was beginning to swell and visitors brought their congratulations to the house each day, Ozeret was robbed of her favorite task. She watched in mute misery as her mistress unlocked the spice cabinet and poured spices into the mortar. She hung her head as the pestle bruised the spices and filled the room with their mysterious smells.

Soon she shrank into a small, dark core of despair.

ONE MORNING, EARLIER than the usual time, the first visitor arrived. When Ozeret took the young woman's cloak, she was surprised to see a gown flecked with blood and hair hanging loose and disheveled.

Ozeret was shocked by the sorrow she saw on the young woman's face and the pain that seemed to constrict her. She watched as her mistress stepped back from her guest and held her at arms' length.

"What troubles you, Elizabeth?" she heard her mistress ask. "When I last saw you, you were a joyful bride. Niece, what has befallen you?"

Her mistress led the young woman to the table and signaled to Ozeret to pour the wine. Then she raised her goblet and said, "May peace fill your heart, Elizabeth, and may you leave your sorrow in this house whose new joy has the strength to take up your burden."

Ozeret listened intently as she sat on her pallet in the corner and her fingers spun fine thread. She watched the young woman try to compose her face as she replied, "My aunt, I bless you in your joy and wish my mother, your beloved older sister, were still alive to see your long-held wish come true. I too pray for a child of my own but instead..."

Then the woman started to sob, and Ozeret could barely make out her words.

"Oh Anne, my dear aunt, there is such trouble that I have no hope at all. I must leave Jerusalem and take with me the disgrace that has fallen on my husband's house."

Ozeret sat motionless, her spinning forgotten, listening to a story more disturbing than the nightmares that robbed her rest.

"I hear the rumors whispered by women who shun me," Elizabeth began, "as I hurry through the streets. I pray that their gossip is false, that my new husband Zachariah was not the man who raped sweet Miriam, his own sister, and caused her womb to ripen before her spirit was ready to leave the innocence of childhood behind.

Aunt, you have felt the scorn of the people of our city. I have always admired you, since I was a young girl, and my mother explained to me why you held your head high and never stopped to talk to the other women in the market or at the well. I couldn't imagine what it would be to live so alone, never joining the family for meals or the Passover celebration. Yet always you greeted me warmly, and when I visited your home with my mother, I saw the love between you and your husband and wanted that love in my own home, even more than I hoped for the child that you could never have. Until now." Elizabeth smiled through her tears.

"But my husband is a cold and violent man, by turns, and I have lost my people too.

No, Aunt. Don't comfort me yet. I must tell you my story. Living as I had, the youngest child with no other children still at home, I had been lonely without knowing it. And then, after watching my mother disappear into the darkness that stole her mind before her body followed, I was eager to escape.

Zachariah took notice of me. My father was glad to have me marry into the priestly caste and leave him to settle into grief with no one but a servant to tend to the empty shell he had become. Soon after I moved into the home of my husband, his sister Miriam came to me, her face ashen, and showed me the blood on her gown. I was surprised she did not know the cause but comforted her and gave her my own strips of linen to catch the flow. She seemed such a child, too young to be a woman, but soon her breasts filled her gown and her face lost its roundness. And yet she still acted like a child, content to do her mother's bidding at home and walk beside me through the city, unaware of the glances of men and boys.

I was charmed by Miriam and found in her the companion I never had and recompense for the difficulties of my marriage.

But then, not a year after I joined the family, Miriam changed. She grew silent and moody and refused to accompany me to the marketplace or the well. I remember you asked me about her when I visited you, Aunt, but I just said she was feeling ill.

And then I realized it had been two months since Miriam had requested the strips of linen that I washed for her because she seemed to me too delicate for such a task. I watched her closely in the days that followed and saw how sparingly she ate and how pale she had become. I pretended to myself that all was well. She was young. Her body was still discovering its rhythms. She was leaving childhood and was not yet the woman she would be.

The weeks went by. Miriam's mother, Hannah, my mother-in-law, chastised her daughter constantly for forgetfulness and carelessness in performing her chores. Miriam's brother, my husband, joined his father in mocking her when she spilled the wine or burned the lentils. And Miriam became more and more silent and sad.

Finally I could fool myself no longer. I took Miriam aside while my husband and father-in-law were at the Temple and my mother-in-law was visiting a neighbor and asked her if she had been with a man.

Aunt, she crawled into my lap and hugged me and cried and cried.

I asked her if she could tell me who he was, and she shook her head. I asked her if she had wanted his attention, and she shook her head even harder. Then she stood up and went back to chopping the onions for the lentil stew, her face covered with tears but not another sound coming from her. I got a cloth and bathed her face and took the knife from her hand. Then I took both of her hands in mine and told her we must tell her mother. She shook her head and whispered, 'I cannot.'

And so that task fell to me.

Her labor was more than her body and spirit could bear. The baby would not turn to face the journey into the world. The agony went on for two days and two nights while the midwife tried to turn him. By the time she succeeded and the baby's head finally appeared, Miriam's hand that had been clutching mine went slack and the room went silent.

Then the midwife began to pull the baby from Miriam's body. She kept stopping to wipe her hands against her shift. They were slick with her sweat and Miriam's blood.

I kept watching Miriam's face, all white and hollowed out but peaceful at last.

The midwife kept grunting as she worked, and then Miriam's mother made the sound I once heard in the hills outside the walls of the city. Do you remember that time, Aunt? It was after our mother died and we had put her in the cave for burial. You were holding my hand, and everyone was walking quietly back to the city gates.

I thought the sound came from me, that terrified cry, but you told me it was the sound a rabbit makes when it is caught and killed. I hadn't known rabbits could make a sound, Aunt, until that day. That cry woke me from nightmares every night for months and months. Sometimes it still does.

Aunt, let me finish. It is a great comfort to put this horror into words for other ears to hear.

After the midwife cut the cord and cleaned and swaddled the infant, Miriam's mother put the infant in my arms and sent the midwife to find a wet nurse. She bathed Miriam's mangled body and covered it with fresh linens. Then, with her authority as grandmother, she put her hand on her grandson's head and spoke into the cold silence of the room.

'I name you Judas,' she said. 'Born under the sign of the scorpion, you have already brought great grief and shame to me and to my family. For this I curse the god of Israel and the man he allowed to cause such harm in this world. But I bless you, son of my only beloved daughter, and I pray to the god of spirit and hope that you be a bearer of light as well as darkness.'

Then she went into her bedroom, and her weeping filled the house.

I lacked the will to build up the fire against the chill of the rainy autumn night. No provision had been made in this house for the baby's comfort or well being. He lay on a corner of the bed with his blue eyes, as blind as a newborn kitten's, wide open. I wrapped my woolen cape around him and then stood in the doorway under the moonless sky waiting for the midwife to return.

Aunt, who was the father? Could the rumors about my husband be true?

Does the god of our people care nothing for women and children? Is he as cold and cruel as my husband?

No, Aunt. I am not quite done or ready for your comfort. Hear me to the end.

I waited by the dying fire with the silent infant and his dead mother until the midwife entered the room with the wet nurse. I knew my husband and my father-in-law would return now that the unclean work of women was done. So I walked through the streets until the night faded and a new day allowed me to come to you.

I leave Jerusalem tomorrow, Aunt. My mother-in-law sends me to the village of Ein Karem to raise her bastard grandson far from this city and to endure my husband as well as I can. If you know a god of mercy, pray for me when I am gone."

Ozeret wept with the women, silent and unseen, as she sat on her pallet in the corner. She wept for the boy named Judas who, like her, would be an outcast in his home.

The cradle gleamed in sunlight that found its way through the narrow street and into the house at this late-morning hour. Despite the chill in the air, Anne had opened the shutters to enjoy the brief passage of autumnal light across the room.

There were now two chests in the bedroom, the one that Anne brought to her marriage and a new chest, beautifully carved by her nephew Joseph. It held the swaddling cloth and baby linens for the child who pressed against her taut belly and was almost ready to insist its way into the world.

Anne could barely lean over to reach the baby's tiny linens where they rested on the fragrant cedar, one wide board planed to a gleaming smoothness under her nephew's strong hands and fastened so seamlessly to the sides of the chest that no insect or rodent could ever enter.

For the past several weeks Anne had stayed in the house, content to let Ozeret fetch water from the well, empty the chamber pot into the gutter, purchase food for their meals, and keep the house in preparation for the arrival of the child. She dozed through the day in her chair by the window and kept Joachim awake most of the night, unable to sleep beside her restless discomfort.

Anne had no stories to tell him to help the long hours pass. Her mind was occupied with thoughts of baby linens and worries about her withered breasts providing milk for her child. She no longer had a quarrel with Joachim's god or concern for Joachim's work in the Temple. She barely noticed when Joachim rubbed her lower back as she lay on her side or helped her from the bed to use the chamber pot. And she took for granted that her servant would free her from all household tasks. Her mind, body, and spirit were in her womb.

Anne's baby arrived on a clear autumn night under a crescent moon and a sky more full of stars than the most learned astrologer could reckon. She emerged so quickly and quietly that Ozeret barely had time to summon the midwife. By the time the sun was brightening the sky, the baby girl was swaddled and resting in her mother's arms.

Ozeret flew through the wakening city to summon her mistress's kinswomen. She saw in their faces and heard in their voices their willingness to share the good fortune that had revived this withered branch of their illustrious family. Ozeret's heart rejoiced for her mistress and master as she led the procession of hastily-dressed women through the streets and into the house whose weeks of hushed expectancy now rang out with the sound of the crying infant. Ozeret held open the curtain for the kinswomen who gathered around the bed to marvel at the delicate head emerging from its swaddling clothes. She felt her mistress's joy as if it were her own when the baby's mouth found her mother's nipple and began to suck. A collective sigh of relief went up from the women. The oldest of them led the wet nurse from the bed chamber. Ozeret watched as she pressed a coin into the woman's hand and sent her on her way. Then Ozeret closed the bedroom curtain and went about her daily tasks.

CHAPTER 3

Jerusalem, three years later

The fig tree swelled with the promise of fruit. Birdsong filled the garden. Ozeret sat quietly in the early dawn allowing her spirit to leave the darkness of sleep and settle into its daytime chamber. She loved the time between night and day when the garden was hers and the streets were still quiet. She wondered where the birds went when the bustle of day began. She never saw them on the garden wall or in the branches of the tree. But she heard them each morning when the weather was warm enough for her to creep out into the garden.

An empty spider web glistened in the faint light, waiting for the creatures in the garden to waken. Ozeret wondered which insect's death would destroy the web's symmetry.

Somewhere a baby started to cry. Ozeret rose from the bench. Glancing down, she saw a scorpion making its way towards the garden wall. She stood watching until it crept through the herbs and crawled up the stones and disappeared. Then she went quietly into the house to begin the day.

As the winter rains relented and spring brought fresh herbs to Jerusalem's markets, Ozeret listened to night after night of talk and crying and negotiations behind the bedroom curtain.

"She is my niece," her mistress pleaded. "Not once have I seen her since she left for Ein Karem. Husband, it is not right that Elizabeth should suffer for the sins of her husband Zachariah, if he is at fault, and for the disgrace of her sister-in-law Miriam who was a guiltless child."

Ozeret heard Joachim plead with his wife.

"Wife, I have barely become accustomed to a place of dignity in my city and in the Temple. I dare not have the scorn that drove Zachariah from the city and demeans him in the eyes of the priests contaminate me. Our daughter Mary regained honor for us. Don't ask me to allow your sister's family to disgrace us once again."

Night after night Ozeret heard her master and her mistress say the same words that carried them to the same place far from each other and the love they shared. Ozeret stroked her hair for comfort and smelled the herbs and spices that perfumed the room and wondered at the loneliness her people made for themselves.

Finally, not a month before the Passover festival would begin, Ozeret heard her master whisper, in a voice of weary resignation, "Thy will be done, Anne. I take your invitation to Zachariah today when I go to the Temple. Prepare yourself and our child for whatever may come of your folly."

Then sounds of lovemaking lulled Ozeret into a dreamless sleep.

THE NEXT DAY Anne's brother Benjamin stormed into the house. Ozeret watched him spit on the floor and heard him curse his sister for inviting Elizabeth into her home. She heard him curse Zachariah and call Judas a piece of filth unworthy to be thrown into the gutter of their city.

Ozeret watched Anne's eyes fill with tears. Her mistress pleaded with Benjamin. She reminded him that Elizabeth was his niece and should be allowed to see her aunt and uncle and cousins. But Benjamin shouted that he and his sons would never break bread with such people.

And so this Passover, Mary's third, would be celebrated without her uncle and her cousins. Instead Ozeret set the table for Zachariah and his mother Hannah and for Elizabeth and the boy named Judas.

By noon the house was spotless. Every trace of leavened bread had been swept and scrubbed away. Ozeret smiled as Mary watched her hide a piece of unleavened bread behind the water jug by the door. This year Mary was old enough to look for the afikomen, and Ozeret wanted to be certain that she would find it quickly and easily.

Ozeret was startled to see the youngest of Benjamin's sons enter the room. Ozeret heard the longing in his voice when he asked if he could give his cousin a Passover gift.

Her mistress smiled and said, "Yes, of course. She's in the garden. But hurry, Joseph. Your father won't want you to be late for Seder."

Joseph rushed out of the room with a wooden box under his arm.

Ozeret heard her mistress whisper to Joachim, "Husband, I fear for Joseph. He seems to grow more tender as he turns into a man, and I know the trouble he has at home with Benjamin and his brothers. How will he find his way in the world?"

"He is eighteen now and in a few years will marry. He has a talent with wood. Once he has a family of his own, he will be fine. You coddle him too much."

Ozeret heard the anger in her mistress's voice as she answered. "He is the youngest of five brothers, and his birth cost him his mother and with her the love of his father. I have tried to give him a little of what he lost."

Ozeret heard Joachim sigh. This was a familiar argument. She wondered why her mistress and her master shaped the same thoughts into words again and again, seeming to forget the divide words made between them.

***OZERET'S WORDS HAD** once cost her both home and family. When she spoke the truth as a child, she was abandoned.*

So now she only spoke when no one heard her. When she knew the house was empty, she walked around the room where food was made and eaten and where she slept. She named the things she handled every day and spoke to them in a voice that matured with her body.

"You are my bowl," she might say. "You are the color of the earth and you are damaged but very strong."

Or "You hold the wine my mistress drinks and are allowed to touch her lips each day."

Or to the cabinet hanging on the wall: "You hold the herbs and spices that turn food and wine into a song and fill the house with fragrance and delight."

Ozeret went into the garden. On the bench below the fig tree Joseph had assembled a caravan of wooden animals. They wound around the curving garden bench, camels and donkeys and sheep and a tiny lamb. Mary stood holding Joseph's hand, with her mouth slightly open, as she looked from one animal to another.

Suddenly Mary cried out. She pointed at the empty wooden box below the bench. Ozeret turned to where the child was pointing. A scorpion crawled out of the box and disappeared behind the fig tree.

Ozeret felt Mary hug her leg. She took the child in her arms and held her. Together they watched as the scorpion eased beyond the tree and disappeared into the shade of the herbs at the edge of the garden.

Ozeret heard footsteps approaching. When she turned, she saw her mistress walking with her arm around a younger woman. Straggling behind was a little boy with bright red hair. His blue eyes darted anxiously around the garden as if he knew he had no place there.

Ozeret was struck by the change three years had made. The younger woman, her mistress's niece Elizabeth, walked heavily. Her dull eyes had dark shadows beneath them. She reminded Ozeret of an old, overburdened donkey.

Ozeret hugged Mary and set her gently on the ground. Then she led the child to Elizabeth.

Elizabeth bent down and embraced the little girl. "You are a miracle child," she whispered to Mary. "Perhaps someday such a miracle will come to me."

Ozeret watched Judas, hoping he hadn't heard. But she saw his eyes harden against the pain of Elizabeth's words, and her heart ached in sympathy. When her mistress and Elizabeth left the garden,

Ozeret knelt between the children, an arm around each one, and helped them begin a game of racing the wooden animals. She stayed with them in the garden until Mary was laughing and Judas, the same age as his cousin but a full head taller, had a smile tugging at one corner of his mouth.

No one noticed the sound of the gate closing behind Joseph.

Ozeret dried the last of the special dishes and goblets and placed them on their shelves. Then she stood at the foot of her pallet and ate the cold food that she had scraped from the Seder plates into her bowl.

She had not saved the food from Zachariah's plate. She was afraid the malice that seemed to outline his tall, thin frame and gaunt face had poisoned the food on his dish and might enter her if she ate from it.

As Ozeret wiped her bowl clean with a scrap of unleavened bread, her finger traced the bowl's familiar crack. She was startled to notice that the crack had widened. She ran her hand slowly over the outside of the bowl. It felt intact.

Ozeret studied the people lingering around the table. Judas, his head barely visible from the depths of an adult's chair, was staring straight ahead. He seemed afraid to move in case he might capture someone's attention. Ozeret kept watching the little boy, holding her breath as she waited for him to blink. Finally he moved his eyes until they found her face. When she smiled at him, he returned her smile. Then he resumed his careful, fearful pose.

Elizabeth was sitting next to Judas, but not once had Ozeret seen her lean over to whisper to him or urge some food upon him. She seemed trapped in the same mute misery as the child.

Joachim sat at the head of the table. He had been silent during the meal, except when the ritual demanded his voice; his eyes spoke his misery.

Judas's grandmother Hannah had barely touched her food or spoken. Her full attention was on Zachariah. Ozeret ached for Hannah, two years a widow, who looked old and frail and seemed to wither as the meal went on and her son sat indifferent to her gaze and her timid stroking of his arm. The only time Hannah spoke was when Zachariah forbade Judas to join Mary in looking for the hidden unleavened bread.

Ozeret saw Elizabeth look up in surprise when she heard her mother-in-law whisper, "He is a child at Seder, my son. It is his role to search for the afikoman with the other child, his cousin, and help to end the feast."

Zachariah's glare silenced Hannah, and Elizabeth lowered her eyes to her plate.

Now little Mary was nodding in her high chair, clutching the half-eaten sweet that had been her reward for finding the afikoman. Ozeret wondered how long these people would sit, each locked in misery, before this feast could end and they could disentangle themselves from each others' presence. She hoped this would be the last Passover that Elizabeth's family would attend in this house and then felt the cruelty of her wish. What must life be for Elizabeth and Judas living with Zachariah? Could they take some small comfort from being in Jerusalem for Passover?

Finally Zachariah rose and bowed to Joachim. Zachariah helped his mother to her feet, and Elizabeth nodded to Judas who scrambled down from his chair and stood waiting. Anne rose and took her sleeping child in her arms. She whispered to Elizabeth, so quietly that Ozeret could not make out her words, and put a hand on Judas's red hair. The boy looked up at her with startled eyes, and Anne smiled down at him.

Zachariah held back as his family slowly filed out into the darkening street. He waited until the curtain closed behind Anne and Mary. Then he spoke to Joachim.

"Your child will be four after the summer, will she not?"

"Yes," Joachim replied.

"You do remember your promise?"

Joachim hung his head and seemed to shrivel up inside his ceremonial robe. Ozeret heard Anne singing Mary to sleep. The lamps on the table sputtered. Finally Joachim looked at Zachariah, his eyes hollow and full of dread, and nodded.

"Yes, Zachariah, I remember. I will repay the miracle of Mary's birth by giving her to the Temple until she is a woman and ready to be betrothed."

Zachariah smiled and bowed and left the room to join his family waiting for him in the darkness.

That night Anne's sobs and cries of rage woke Mary who cried along with her mother. Ozeret listened in horror as Joachim told his wife of the promise he had made to the god of Israel and the priests of the Temple.

"You cannot take her from me," Anne screamed. "She does not belong to you or to your god. She is mine."

Joachim's voice was muffled by the sobs of Anne and Mary. Then, finally, there was silence.

Ozeret stood watching *an enormous serpent twine down the fig tree in the garden. Its head, resting on the garden bench, had the delicate face of Mary. The serpent's eyes, brown and innocent, were fixed on a scorpion creeping stealthily down the garden wall. The scorpion stopped and turned its head towards Ozeret. Its eyes held her paralyzed in their gaze. Then the scorpion resumed its journey down the wall and disappeared beneath a rosemary bush.*

When Ozeret could move again, she looked at the fig tree. The serpent had disappeared. Ozeret's silent screams shook the leaves of the tree.

Ozeret woke from her nightmare and lay panting in the silence of the room. The air hung heavy with the smell of crushed rosemary.

Spring passed and summer. The cisterns gaped empty, waiting for the rains to come, and all of Jerusalem felt dusty and dry.

Joseph entered his aunt's garden through the alley gate. He watched his cousin Mary for a few minutes, hoping for her to notice him and run to him with her arms outstretched so he could lift her and spin her around. But she continued to sit very still on the bench under the fig tree with her hands folded in her lap and her eyes staring straight ahead.

A gust of wind swept through the garden, shaking the last of the fig leaves to the ground. Joseph went to Mary and wrapped his cape around her as she shivered on the bench.

"What is it, little cousin?" Joseph asked.

Mary turned her face up to his. "I go to live in the Temple," she said, speaking with her usual precocious care and precision. "Father is talking to the priests."

Joseph felt as if the bench were cracking beneath him. He started to get up. He wanted to find Joachim.

Joseph felt Mary's cold small hand on his. He forced himself to breathe deeply, the way he did at home when the clamor of his brothers and the orders of his father closed in on him. Then he looked down at his cousin and made himself smile.

"Your father has promised you to the Temple priests?" he asked. Mary nodded, her brown eyes full of tears.

Joseph took her hand and led her into the house. He sat on the floor beside her and helped her build a tower with the blocks he had carved for her fourth birthday.

His aunt was crying behind the bedroom curtain. The servant was spinning thread on her pallet in the corner of the room. The room felt cold, and there was no smell of cooking though the time for the midday meal was near.

When Mary knocked over the tower they had built together, Joseph stood up and left the house.

Soon he found himself sitting under a gnarled tree on the Mount of Olives, staring down at the city. The Temple on its proud hill dominated the skyline. What would become of little Mary in that place?

Joseph stood up and wiped his eyes. He went to work sawing branches from the ancient olive tree, sturdy limbs that he would fashion into walking sticks to sell in the family's shop in the street below the Temple. Cold autumn sun made the sawdust glisten and gleam as it danced to the ground. The beauty of the afternoon mocked his despair.

For as long as he could remember he had wanted to escape from the city with its priests and Roman soldiers and his father's harsh rule. Whenever he could find an excuse to leave his father's workshop, he went to the home of his aunt where he was warmed by her smile and the gentleness of her husband and, for the last four years, the miracle of little Mary who laughed her delight to see him and the toys he carved for her.

Sometimes he would happen upon the little girl holding the hand of her mother or her mother's servant, a deaf and speechless creature of about his own age. Mary kept her eyes fixed on her tiny sandals as she walked, but her face would light up when Joseph spoke her name. Then she dropped the hand she was holding and ran to him. Joseph would lift her to his shoulder and carry her to her home, risking the blows of his father for being late in returning from whatever errand took him from his father's workshop.

Joseph dreaded the years ahead of him. His aunt would lose heart after giving up the one thing she had most longed for.

Her home would become a place of despair instead of refuge. And his cousin, the gift that had come so unexpectedly and had given him such hope and joy, would be hidden in one of the hundreds of rooms in the Temple complex, far from her home and garden and the people who loved her. What would become of her? And how would he survive this loss?

Joseph tried and failed to lose himself in the rhythm of the saw. One memory was especially insistent.

He was pulling a fat worm from the dirt under the bench in Mary's garden. He loved to hear her laugh when a worm tickled its way across her tiny outstretched palm. Suddenly, out of the corner of his eye, he noticed a black scorpion crawling from a crack in the leg of the bench. Its tail was within striking distance of Mary's bare foot. Joseph scooped his little cousin up so suddenly that she began to cry in fright. Mary cried even harder when he smashed the scorpion with his sandal. His aunt rushed into the garden and took the sobbing child from his arms.

That day, as Joseph walked slowly home, he was afraid he had lost his little cousin's trust by killing one of the creatures in her garden. But after Passover she accepted the intricate scorpion he carved for her and forgave him with her smile.

Soon she would be beyond his love and protection.

Joseph tried to bury his despair before returning to his father's home and the taunting scrutiny of his brothers. And so he stayed on the hillside until the sky darkened and the olive tree was stripped of all its limbs.

Ozeret fastened the child's cape and picked up her small bag with its change of linens. The Temple would provide a pallet and blanket and a bowl and cup for meals. Mary had pleaded with her father to be allowed to take the wooden scorpion Joseph carved for her, but Joachim had told her, gently but firmly, that toys were not allowed in the place where she was going. Since that argument, the first time Mary had tried to assert her will, the child had been silent and distant.

Her mother too was silent as they walked from the house to the Temple complex. She tried to hug her child before they left the house, but Mary stood as still and unresponsive as her high chair sitting empty and now useless at the table. Anne's face, already eerily pale and shadowed, lost the last vestiges of color and life. She straightened and left the room.

Ozeret followed her master and mistress up the hill. The space between them seemed to hold the chill of winter though the autumn sun was warm and the sky a deeper blue than the cape Mary had to leave behind. Her Temple clothes were all of unbleached linen.

Mary's hand felt limp and cold, but she walked steadily up the hill. Ozeret remembered a walk like this, many years ago, with her own hand in her father's and a feeling of shame and confusion and desolation blotting out the hills as they walked away from her home towards the city of Jerusalem. She knew the child needed to find her own strength and courage so she kept her own eyes looking straight ahead and tried to neither think nor feel until this deed was done.

OZERET STOOD IN the courtyard of the house. The cistern was full, as high as she had ever seen it.

If only the rain would stop. Her mistress sat huddled in bed all day, refusing to leave except to use the chamber pot. In the evening Joachim returned from the Temple looking like one of the bedraggled cats who used to seek refuge in Ozeret's alley when the rain came down in thick, cold sheets and every creature with a home or hole to call its own disappeared from the streets of the city.

Ozeret barely had to lower the water jug. Raindrops danced on the surface of the water and dampened her cloak.

Her cloak hadn't felt dry for days. After Joachim went to bed each night, she spread his cloak and hers over chairs set in front of the stove and added extra dry dung to the fire. But they still felt damp when she woke each morning and stirred the fire to heat water for her mistress.

***OZERET LOOKED FORWARD** to the day when the rain would stop and the sky would brighten. Then she could see herself in the cistern's water. Looking at her reflection she would pretend she had a friend, a young woman with eyes as dark as her hair and eyebrows that almost met above her nose. Ozeret's friend had a mouth wider than the mouth of her mistress and with fuller lips. When she smiled at her friend, her friend smiled back, unashamed of her missing teeth. Ozeret's friend remembered the blow that sent the teeth into Ozeret's throat where she gagged on them and blood and her own tears until, finally, her mother raised her up and pounded her on the back until the teeth flew out and Ozeret could breathe again.*

SHE CARRIED THE jug of water from the courtyard and poured it into the pot on the stove. Then she hung her cloak on its peg.

Ozeret waited for the water to warm so she could sponge off her mistress. She wished Anne would use the bath room. Ozeret wondered what it felt like to sit in warm water and wash with the lavender-scented soap Joachim brought home as a gift for his wife.

Once Anne allowed Ozeret to bathe Mary in the bath room. Little Mary's unwashed body had begun to make the house stink, and Anne was too tired from a cold to bathe the child by herself. Anne sat on a stool next to the tub with Mary in her lap and tapped Ozeret's arm when the height and heat of the water were perfect. Then Ozeret took Mary from Anne and removed her shift and the linens that caught her dirty business. She lifted the little girl into the warm, fragrant water and washed her carefully as the child splashed and laughed and looked from her mother to Ozeret waiting for their approval and delight.

Maybe the bath room reminded her mistress of Mary. But then every room in the house still held reminders. Mary's high chair was tucked under the table. Her blue cloak, its precious dye extracted from the glands of sea snails and worth its weight in gold, hung by the door. And the trundle bed that Joseph had built to replace her cradle was pushed under the bed, still made up with the linens Anne had spun and sewn. There was no escaping Mary, much as Ozeret wished she could.

After the sad walk to the Temple and the return home and the silent meal that neither Anne nor Joachim touched, Ozeret had scraped their plates into her bowl, eaten her fill, and hoped that her life would go back to the way it was before Mary arrived. She hoped that she would hear her mistress and master tell stories at night and delight in their love for each other without fearing that they would disturb the child sleeping beside them. She hoped that her mistress would leave her in peace to prepare the meals without fussing about making special dishes for the child. She hoped that she could do the weekly wash without having her mistress interfere to be sure Ozeret rinsed all the soap from Mary's soiled linens. And most of all she hoped that the gnawing feeling in her heart, the pain she felt when she looked at the child who was so praised and coddled and loved by her own master and mistress, would end when the child was gone.

At last the rains ended. Ozeret felt mildewed and moldy after the months trapped in the dark, gloomy house. Their visitors had been few. Anne's misery was so profound and her blasphemy so outspoken that the relatives who had once filled the house to celebrate Mary's arrival now shunned Anne, just as they had before the miracle of her pregnancy. Anne railed, to anyone who would listen, against the god of the Temple and his priests who had sacrificed her child to a room hidden in the Courtyard of the Women. Only Joseph still braved the dismal house and sat holding his aunt's hand as she rested in her bed with the curtain pulled open. Together they sat in silent misery, comforted, Ozeret supposed, by each other's understanding of the great wrong that had occurred.

At first, Joachim tried to reason with his wife. He reminded her of all the special sacrifices the chief priest had allowed him to make, pleading with their god to give them a child. He implored her to accept the honorable place Mary had won them among their people and to wait for her to become a woman and leave the Temple. He pictured for her the day Anne herself had sacrificed two doves in the Courtyard of Women in thanks for the birth of her child. She had been happy then and at one with his god and priests and the Temple.

But Anne was beyond reason or consolation. Ozeret guessed that Joachim was as relieved as she when her mistress sunk into an apathetic torpor and, if not peace, at least there was quiet in the house.

Ozeret went about her daily tasks keeping the house and her mistress clean and in good order and preparing meals that were fragrant with herbs and spices.

With the garden too sodden to enjoy, the spice cabinet became for Ozeret her only solace. She was profligate in pounding and grinding and almost giddy in her freedom to point to an empty box or jar and know that Joachim would return that evening with replacements from the markets in the Upper City near the Temple where the priests and wealthy Romans sent their servants to shop.

And so the autumn and winter passed until finally Ozeret could squat in the alley without rain pounding down on her head and the fig tree in the garden grew leaves and swelling buds of fruit.

As the rain stopped and the sky brightened, Anne seemed to shed her darkness and crawl back into her new, hard life without her child. She joined her husband for the evening meal and smiled her appreciation to Ozeret when she scooped the fragrant stew onto her bread and sipped her spicy wine. She spoke to her husband behind the curtain in the darkness and cried quietly, the sound muffled by Joachim's embrace.

And then, one morning, Anne announced to Joachim that she and Ozeret would travel the next day to Ein Karem to visit her niece Elizabeth.

Joachim paused in the doorway and looked at her in astonishment. Anne smiled calmly at him. "Zachariah instructs the girls in the Temple, does he not?" she said. "You see him from time to time but, being a man, elicit no news of our little Mary. I will implore Zachariah to tell me if she is taller and if she smiles and whether she is plump and rosy. And if he will not speak with me about our daughter, I will implore Elizabeth to find out what she can."

Ozeret watched Joachim, wondering how he would react to this extraordinary announcement. She felt a twinge of sympathy for Mary. Being instructed by Zachariah must be an additional misery for her. Then she thought of the little boy, Judas. Her mistress hadn't mentioned him. Ozeret wondered if he was as unnoticed in his home as she in hers.

All that day, while Ozeret packed clothes and food for the journey, her mistress rushed in and out of the house. She came back with gifts for her niece: a bolt of crimson linen, a jar of fragrant ointment, a package of precious saffron.

Anne brought home a bedraggled boy to lead the donkey. Through the open window Ozeret heard her order him to sleep in the little stable on a pile of straw that night.

Anne summoned Ozeret to the bath house to wash her hair and rub her feet with a pumice stone and massage them with lavender ointment.

After supper, she sent Ozeret to the stable with some bread and cheese for the boy who was obediently perched on the straw next to the donkey. Then she watched while Ozeret filled the donkey's panniers with food and clothes and the gifts for Elizabeth.

That night Ozeret lay on her pallet, exhausted but too excited to sleep. She would soon be out of the city and back in the hills she had travelled with her father so many years ago. She had been too young and terrified to notice much as her father dragged her along the path. But now she remembered colors and smells that were foreign to the city where she had grown to be a woman. She remembered hills spread out as far as her eyes could see. And she felt her heart expand with joy as she rubbed her hair against her cheek and imagined herself on a journey.

CHAPTER 4

Ein Karem

Ozeret stumbled behind the donkey and her dozing mistress, tripping over rocks and rises in the path as she looked around her. Even the donkey was walking with her ears pricked and her eyes and nostrils wide.

Ozeret wondered if the skinny, pale boy leading the donkey had ever been beyond the city walls, but then she was distracted by the fragrance of herbs. Here in the Judean hills, as the day was warming under a brilliant blue sky, the rosemary and thyme and oregano that so delighted her in the spice cabinet at home smelled deeper and stronger and so alive that she almost shouted her joy. The hills were blanketed with brilliant wildflowers set off by the greens and grays of herbs and grasses, and birdsong drifted from bushes and the occasional tree.

Ozeret felt as intoxicated as that night when she secretly drank a goblet of spiced wine to dispel the grief and gloom hanging so heavy in the house. But this feeling was better. Her head spun and her heart raced, but with brightness instead of the confusion and leaden feeling the wine had given her.

Soon the village appeared, a jumble of houses hugging the hillside with smoke from cooking fires rising lazily in the still air.

Zachariah's house was on the outskirts of the village near a footpath that led up into the high pasture where he grazed his flock of sheep. Joachim had assured Anne that they would know it by the bee hives Elizabeth kept on the edge of a patch of wildflowers beside the house.

When Anne saw the house with its flowers and hives, she ordered the boy to stop the donkey and help her down. Her bones creaked noisily as she straightened her knees and back, and Ozeret saw pain line her face before she willed it away and composed herself for the visit. By the time Elizabeth appeared in the doorway, Anne was smiling and her arms were outstretched to embrace her niece.

Ozeret looked around the room and saw that the shelf for plates and goblets and the doors of the spice cabinet were plain and unadorned. But in the middle of the table an earthenware jug of wildflowers and herbs brought the spring morning inside, and the air that crept through the open window and door buzzed with the industry of bees. Ozeret felt memory tugging at her, another room with flowers and sweet, fresh air. Then fear took hold and the flowers seemed to wither and the air smelled rank. She reached out for the door frame to steady herself and closed her eyes.

When she opened them, Ozeret saw Elizabeth pulling out a chair for her mistress and heard a scrambling noise from under the table. Elizabeth called out sharply, "Judas, come out this minute."

The little boy appeared slowly, calloused heels first and then his backside and finally a head of matted red hair. He crawled out with his face down and then slowly stood up, keeping his back to the table. To Ozeret who stood facing him as she leaned against the door frame, he seemed too tall for his four years and his face too thin for early childhood.

Judas ignored Elizabeth's request that he greet her aunt and instead fixed his pale blue eyes on Ozeret. Then he said, "I want to eat outside."

Ozeret heard Elizabeth's exasperated sigh. She turned to her aunt and complained, "I can't control him. Only Zachariah can bend his will. When he's in Jerusalem, the boy does whatever he wants and when Zachariah's here, Judas cowers like a mongrel in the dusty streets of the village trying to dodge my husband's temper."

Ozeret heard her mistress murmur something soothing. Elizabeth nodded and got up to wrap three pieces of bread and some cheese in a cloth. Then she told Judas, "Go with the servant and find a place to eat your meal. You are to share the food." Elizabeth handed the bundle of food to Ozeret and then returned to the table to confide her woes to her aunt.

Judas darted out the door and past the bee hives and up the path that led up to Zachariah's pasture. Ozeret signaled to the donkey boy and hurried after Judas.

She found him a few minutes later perched on a large, flat boulder by the side of the path. Her sandals crushed wild thyme that grew around the spot Judas had chosen. The air smelled pungent and alive. She watched the boy tie the donkey to an old, gnarled olive tree and pointed to the water flask. He brought it to her. Ozeret uncorked the flask and drank.

A memory came to Ozeret. She saw a woman kneeling by a spring with her hands cupped to catch the water. The woman held her hands up to a little girl's mouth, and the child drank the sweet water.

Ozeret tapped Judas on the arm. He fixed her with his strange blue eyes. She pointed from the flask to the hillside, and he smiled his understanding. "The spring is there," he said.

Judas ran up the narrow path. Ozeret followed him and saw that water trickled from a crevice in the rocks. She knelt down and cupped her hands to drink. The water tasted like moss and sunlight. It washed away the staleness of the water in the flask. She smiled her thanks to Judas then covered her mouth with its missing teeth. But Judas was already gone. Ozeret led the donkey to the spring and watched her drink her fill. Then she led the donkey back and tied her once again to the olive tree.

Ozeret heard Judas chattering to the boy, telling him about the creatures that lived under the rocks and the sheep that grazed on the hillside and the honey that the bees made for him to eat. The boy sat on the rock staring hungrily at the bundle of food. Ozeret opened the bundle and handed Judas and the donkey boy their bread and some cheese. Judas took his bread and began to turn it into crumbs that lured a procession of ants up the path.

Ozeret settled herself on the rock and ate her own bread and cheese and smelled the thyme and allowed the sun to lull her into a place half waking and half asleep.

When she returned to the house, her mistress and Elizabeth were still deep in conversation with their meal untouched on their plates. Anne rose from the table when she noticed Ozeret in the doorway. She went outside and instructed the boy that he was to return the donkey to Jerusalem. The boy's dull eyes showed a brief flicker of fear. Ozeret imagined him spending the rest of the afternoon and part of the evening alone on the path. She wondered how he would find his way back to the donkey's stable once he passed through the gate to the city. The donkey seemed far more alert than the boy. Perhaps she would guide him.

Ozeret went into the house and caught the attention of Elizabeth. She pointed from the bread that lay untouched on the table to the boy standing in the yard. Elizabeth nodded her permission. Ozeret took the bread to the boy. He tucked it under the donkey's blanket and led the donkey back onto the path they had travelled a few hours before.

Elizabeth came out into the yard and led her aunt to the bee hives. They walked arm in arm with their uncovered heads close together, one streaked with gray, the other gleaming black.

Ozeret went into the house and wondered where to scrape the food. She missed her bowl with its familiar crack. The wildflowers on the table had wilted in the afternoon heat.

Ozeret felt something tickle its way across her big toe. She jumped back. Judas scrambled out from under the table and pointed at the scorpion. Ozeret raised her foot. She cringed as her sandal crushed the scorpion. Judas smiled at her and ran out the door.

CHAPTER 5

The Temple in Jerusalem

Mary was afraid of Zachariah, the only priest who came to the room in the Temple where the girls ate and slept and spent their days. He told them stories about sin and despair. He taught them that they had a duty to do whatever their priests and fathers and husbands demanded to atone for their evil natures.

Mary tried to remember the stories her mother told. Her mother taught her that she was a gift from the god of goodness and mercy and that her birth had made love real in the world. Her father treated her like the precious gift her mother described. He never accused her of having an evil nature or being a bearer of sin.

The older girls said that Zachariah's wife was her cousin. Mary wondered how they knew. It made her head ache. She felt as if Zachariah spoiled the memory of her home just like lentils spoiled her bread if they touched it on her plate.

At first Mary despaired of learning. She was too short to weave. Sarah, the older girl who shared her bed, laughed when Mary jumped up and then peered under the loom, trying to reach the shuttle. Finally the old servant, whom the girls called Mattie, walked over to the loom and shook Sarah's arm. "You take care of that little one," she ordered. "You all be kind to the little girls," she added in a low, powerful voice as she stared down each of the older girls. "The way you treat these little ones is the way you're going to be treated someday."

After that Sarah taught her how to spin. At home Mary had often sat on the servant's pallet and watched. Sometimes Ozeret put her hands over Mary's and together they would work the magic that turned the messy wool into beautiful, even thread. Mary learned so quickly that Sarah bragged about her to the other girls and to Mattie. Mary felt happy then.

One night, soon after she came to live at the Temple, Mary woke in the unfamiliar darkness of the girls' sleeping quarters. On this night all the girls had stayed awake, long after Mattie was snoring loudly on her corner pallet, listening to the older girls describe the home of the chief priest where they had danced at a festival the night before. Mary had trouble imagining a room with pictures painted on the walls and furniture painted so it gleamed like gold.

When the room finally settled into the sleep of tired young bodies, Mary lay awake, troubled by the strangeness of her new life and the stories the older girls carried from the world outside the Temple. Finally she slipped out of her pallet, being careful not to disturb Sarah, and crept through the doorway to the courtyard where the cistern caught water and the girls were allowed an hour outside each day during fair weather.

A pale crescent of moonlight shone on the paving stones, and the patch of sky above the courtyard was bright with stars. Mary pulled herself up to the edge of the cistern and peered down. Stars glittered in the water and she imagined herself falling into an upside-down sky. That frightened her, so she lowered herself back down to the cold stones of the courtyard and stood shivering in the chilly autumn air.

She began to warm herself by spinning. As her body turned, her loneliness and fear were replaced by a great spiral of joy that coursed through her from deep within the earth below the courtyard stones. She twirled faster and faster in the moonlit courtyard, barely conscious of her movement or of her white tunic describing a circle around her as she spun.

The pain of her arm, nearly wrenched out of its socket, transformed her ecstasy into terror. Zachariah loomed above her, his fingers bruising the arm he held imprisoned to stop her dance. She could feel his rage and disgust and heard his angry voice, though she was too frightened to understand his words. Then all was darkness.

Mary woke to the face of Mattie bending over her. The moon had moved beyond the courtyard's sky, but the stars still glittered coldly. Mattie lifted Mary and carried her back into the room where the girls lay sleeping. She rocked her gently until the shaking stopped and then tucked her under the blanket on the pallet where Sarah lay snoring quietly.

From that night on Mary felt Zachariah's rage and disgust crouching inside her ready to pounce whenever she began to lose herself in the rhythm of the spindle or the movement of a dance or the pleasure of the scent of olive blossoms in the courtyard. She worked hard at her lessons and kept to herself, never confiding her fears to anyone.

The years slowly passed. Mary grew tall and became one of the older girls with a little novice who slept beside her and learned from her the ways of Temple life.

One night after Mattie, now crippled with arthritis and nearly blind, was snoring loudly in her corner, news of a secret meeting traveled up and down the double row of pallets. Soon all eighteen girls sat around Ruth, the only girl older than Mary, their blankets pulled tightly around them against the damp that seeped through their night shifts from the cold paving stones. The eyes of Ruth's charge, little Naomi, peered sleepily out of the blanket below Ruth's chin. Ruth's long, narrow face was alive with malicious excitement.

"Our rabbi has been struck dumb," Ruth whispered. Then she looked straight at Mary and grinned wickedly. "Your old cousin Elizabeth is pregnant, Mary. Maybe Zachariah is so surprised to finally be a father he's speechless."

Mary felt shock spread among the older girls. Though no one liked their teacher, still he was a priest and such disrespect had been beyond their ken until now. But then the laughter began.

Mary felt sick with shame and so lonely that the force of it swept through like a gust of icy air. She gathered up her little charge and carried her back to their pallet. There she sank deeply into her own thoughts, shutting out the murmur of gossip and muted laughter from Ruth's corner of the room.

She had no memory of Zachariah's wife Elizabeth. She barely even remembered her mother and father, though she glimpsed them three times a year when they walked past her through the corridor that opened into the courtyard of the high altar. The Temple girls and boys, dressed in ceremonial robes of bleached white linen and arranged according to their height and sex, lined the passageway. The smallest children came first; the tallest stood at the entrance to the courtyard where the high altar gleamed and towered in the distance.

As Mary grew older and taller, she moved closer to the high altar, with her hands clasped together and well hidden in the sleeves of the robe that seemed to grow along with her. The hood of the robe shadowed her face and made her feel invisible. Yet each time the wives of the Temple priests followed their husbands through the passageway, Mary felt her mother's eyes seek her out and find her. Mary closed her own eyes then and kept them closed until she felt her mother pass.

Mary woke from a confusion of nightmares to a stickiness between her legs and a fishy smell, unlike the familiar stench of the youngest girls' nighttime accidents. She remembered Ruth's stories about the unclean blood that would curse each of the girls when their time to leave had come.

Mary listened for Mattie's snoring to cease and the room to brighten. Then she tiptoed over to the old woman and whispered her news.

CHAPTER 6

Ein Karem

Elizabeth rose to an urgent need for the chamber pot. The baby pressing against her bladder was waking her several times a night.

Even after all these years of exile from Jerusalem, she observed the custom of attending to her body's needs inside the house rather than squatting over a hole behind the cypress trees where Zachariah and her nephew Judas did their business.

The room was brightening but Zachariah still lay snoring beside her, his morning breath fouling the air.

As Elizabeth steadied herself over the chamber pot, with one hand on the edge of the bed and the other lifting her night shift, she recalled, as she did each morning, the miracle that had found her in this place.

At first Elizabeth *had attributed the waxing and waning of two moons, without the flow of blood, to her thirty-two years. Her womb was drying up and besides, although Zachariah still used her body to relieve his urges, the ritual felt so cold and inhuman to Elizabeth, like all Zachariah's rituals and observances, that she had trouble imagining he could have caused a quickening of life. Then one morning, as* *she sat near the window where gentle April light was brightening the sky, the knowledge came to her.*

All was still. Zachariah was sleeping without his accustomed noisy snores. The bees had not yet left their hives, and even the birds were silent.

Perhaps it was the sunlight that told her, the same light that warmed the earth and caused the hills to riot with color. The light that sent her bees out to gather pollen and bring back to her hives the sweetness of every flower and plant that felt their dancing feet. The light that greened the pastures and caused the lambs to leap so happily that even Judas had to smile.

AS ELIZABETH PULLED her gown over her protruding belly and carried the pot outside, she remembered the flutter below her navel and the beam of light that shimmered around her the morning when she first knew she was with child.

HER SHOUT OF *joy had woken Zachariah. "What is it?" he asked petulantly, shuffling his way through the curtain and into the sun-drenched room where Elizabeth sat by the window. "You woke me with your unseemly noise."*

That morning Elizabeth had dared to laugh at Zachariah's familiar scowl. She rose and went to her husband, taking his hand and placing it on her belly. "Husband, feel the life within me. You are to know the honor of being a father."

Zachariah pulled his hand away and stared in disgust at Elizabeth. "Woman," he spat. "I see barren flesh and feel a stomach rumbling from ill-prepared food." Then he stomped out of the room to relieve himself behind the house.

ELIZABETH RETURNED TO the bed chamber to put the pot under the bed.

The room smelled foul from Zachariah's breath and the peculiar odor that lived in his flesh even after he bathed. She stared at him for a moment. Ever since that morning, months before, when Zachariah denied the miracle that had come to them, he had lost both the power of speech and the power to frighten her.

Elizabeth had taken to praying to Zachariah's god, prayers of thanksgiving for the punishment of her husband and the gift of hope to her. The words formed themselves in her heart and spoke in her mind.

Sometimes she gave voice to her prayers and watched Zachariah's face contort as he struggled to rebuke her for speaking to his god in words of her own. But her swollen belly seemed to stop Zachariah's fist when he tried to strike her, just as his denial of the miracle in her womb had stopped his speech.

Sometimes Elizabeth wondered what Judas thought about the coming child. Judas had grown tall and thin, with a narrow, angular face and his mother's hair, the auburn streaked with gold. His hair and his pale blue eyes set him apart from the other villagers almost as much as the rumored disgrace of his birth fourteen years before.

For the past four years, during the late spring and all the summer months until the rains began in the fall, Judas stayed alone high up in the hills above the village where the pasture was richest and a stream held water throughout the summer.

To her shame, Elizabeth was glad to have him gone. She savored the days when Zachariah discharged his duties in the Temple and Judas was with his uncle's flock. She found peace then, in her lonely exile, tending to her bees and gathering herbs and flowers under a sky almost frightening in its pure, unchanging blue.

In the winter and during shearing time in spring, when the flock stayed close to the village and both Zachariah and Judas were at home, Elizabeth felt trapped inside the room where she prepared their meals and spun thread for their clothes and watched as Judas chafed under the bullying and abuse of her husband.

The baby kicked, and Elizabeth forgot about everything but the life that grew within her.

Judas stretched out on the rocky hillside and closed his eyes against the April sunlight. He remembered when Zachariah first took him up to the summer pasture four years before. Judas had walked behind his uncle and his uncle's flock as the sky brightened and turned shades of red and orange and then a cloudless blue.

That day, while Judas and his uncle bathed their feet in the stream and ate their lunch of bread and cheese, a lamb went missing. Zachariah told Judas to mind the flock and went off into the hills.

Judas watched all day and into the evening. He walked among his uncle's flock as the sun went down. By the time his uncle returned with the hungry lamb bleating for its mother, the moon had risen. The grass on the hillside looked velvety and almost blue in the moonlight, and the stream gleamed as it flowed towards the village.

Zachariah carried the lamb to its mother and watched as it found her teat and sucked in greedy pleasure. Then he sat by the stream to bathe his feet.

Judas sat beside him and felt peace instead of fear in his uncle's presence. As the moon rose and the shadows receded, his uncle told him that the stream went underground and travelled a secret path until it fed the spring in the village below.

Judas sat in silence under the moon. His mind followed the stream on its mysterious path below the surface until it miraculously reappeared as the village spring where his aunt went for water.

Then his uncle rose and Judas followed him and the flock back down to the village.

The next day was the Sabbath. The sheep stayed in their pen. Judas felt fear return as he sat in the village synagogue and smelled the stale bodies all around him. But he remembered the stream that flowed unseen from the peaceful pasture.

During that summer, Judas's tenth, Zachariah taught Judas how to guard the flock and lead it safely up and down the rocky hillside path. During Judas's eleventh summer, his uncle rarely visited the summer pasture to check on Judas. Now that Judas was fourteen, the summer pasture was his own domain.

Judas still found peace by the stream. He liked to sit beside it and bathe his feet. He liked to walk down the stream, to the place where it disappeared into a crevice between two rocks, and then, in his imagination, to follow its hidden course below caves and rocks and the narrow path to the village. His stream fed the spring that filled the jugs of the village women each evening. It ran through rock-lined ditches to the hillside orchards and vineyards and olive trees that fed the people of Ein Karem. His stream made him feel connected to Ein Karem and its people in a way he never felt when he had to live in his uncle's house in the village.

In past years Zachariah insisted that the sheep stay close to home until the riot of spring wildflowers had subsided and the upper pastures were fully established for a long season of summer grazing. Only then would he order Judas to shear the sheep and drive them up into the hills. But this year Judas was going to bring the flock to pasture whenever he pleased. He doubted that Zachariah would come looking for him. Besides, what would Zachariah do if he managed the long, steep climb from the village to the pasture? Stand glaring at Judas and moving his mouth soundlessly and waving his fist? Judas laughed out loud, causing a ewe grazing nearby to raise her head, as he thought of his uncle's silence and his aunt's new joy.

That fist, however, still hovered over the pallet in the little hut Judas had built beside the upper pasture. Even while he slept, Judas felt that fist strike him on the side of the head when he forgot a chore or failed to memorize a verse or perfectly copy a passage from his uncle's scrolls.

Once when he was very young, still capable of hope and the desire to please, Judas tried copying the verses his uncle assigned him using his left hand. To his astonishment and relief, he could control the size and shape of the words and make them march in an even line across the parchment from right to left. His heart lightened and he worked quickly and confidently, waiting for his uncle to look up and see what he had accomplished.

When Zachariah saw what Judas was doing, he carefully took the pen from his hand and set it on its stand. Then he pushed Judas off the stool and kicked him in the ribs.

"You use the hand that wipes your filthy excrement to write the holy words, you foul pig," Zachariah screamed. He kept kicking Judas until Elizabeth threw herself on the boy.

That afternoon Judas and Elizabeth, both limping, walked slowly to the spring to fill the household jug. Elizabeth waited quietly, as always, for the other women to finish and leave. Then she filled her jug and started back home.

After supper that night, before his aunt finished her chores and went behind the curtain to her bedroom, Judas whispered, "Tell me why. Why are we always alone?"

Elizabeth stopped and looked at him. He studied her face for clues. She looked anxious and sad. That frightened him. But he also felt a sense of power. He had her attention.

Elizabeth was quiet for what felt like a long time. Judas listened to his uncle snoring behind the curtain. Finally his aunt spoke.

"Sit down at the table, Judas. You're eight years old. It's time you knew your story."

His aunt talked for a long time. Judas watched her lips moving and tried to listen, but he couldn't take in what she was telling him. All he remembered from her story, after she extinguished the lamp and disappeared behind the curtain, was that he should not have been born.

***THAT NIGHT JUDAS** dreamed of a scorpion stinging a girl as she lay dying in a bloody bed. When Judas woke, he felt the scorpion's tail curled inside him and with it a new danger more powerful than his uncle's fist. He, Judas, carried within him the sting of death. He had killed his mother.*

CHAPTER 7

Jerusalem

Through the passage of seasons becoming ten years, while an empty chair and bed awaited Mary's return, Ozeret was content to be as indispensable and invisible as the pot over the fire or the pestle that ground her mistress's fragrant herbs and spices. She cooked and learned to count and kept the space and objects in her world clean and in good order.

After Anne's furious grief subsided and her love for Joachim returned, Ozeret listened as her mistress whispered her plans for the future to her husband while they lay behind the curtain before sleep. Ozeret imagined the family Anne described, father, mother, and daughter, sitting around the table. They would delay as long as possible Mary's betrothal, Anne whispered to her husband, and even after she married, they would see her every day.

When the long-awaited word from the Temple arrived, Ozeret followed her master and mistress, bowed with age and the weight of a dream becoming real, as they walked slowly past the shops that lined the base of the Temple Mount and ascended the stairs to the Temple. She stood waiting behind them as the priest muttered his prayers of departure and release over the slight figure kneeling before him in the unbleached linen tunic and cloak that were the uniform of Temple girls. Then the girl rose and turned to face her parents.

Ozeret studied Mary from the safety of the black hood of her cloak. The girl's face had the same brow and cheeks as her mother's, though paler and unlined. But her mouth was thinner and her eyes less bright. Ozeret could not read Mary's face or her heart, and when she shifted her gaze to her mistress, she couldn't read her face or heart either. Ozeret felt desolation creep towards her as stealthily as a feral cat.

Her master motioned to the basket that held Mary's possessions. Ozeret picked it up and walked home behind the silence of the re-united family.

Her mistress seemed baffled by the thin, pale girl who sat at her table and slept in the trundle bed beside her. The regular flow of morning into afternoon, with its unspoken round of movements so familiar that they happened without thought, lost their ease and grace. The girl must be considered. What would she like to eat? What would she like to say? What would she like to do?

Ozeret heard her mistress snap at her master when he left the house without a formal farewell to his daughter. He in turn accused her of always criticizing, he who had, night after night, listened to her argue about his god and his beliefs without feeling in any way diminished in his home or in her heart.

Now her mistress complained querulously to her husband and her daughter when Ozeret failed to anticipate the new rhythm of tasks in the house, a rhythm that couldn't settle into a pattern but instead kept changing and shifting according to the changes and shifts in her mistress's moods. Each time her mistress complained about the stupidity and obstinacy of her servant, Ozeret felt herself grow more clumsy and inept. She burned the lentils and cracked the water jug and even left the spice cabinet door ajar, causing Mary to walk dreamily into its corner and acquire a small egg-shaped bump on her smooth, pale brow.

Her mistress had never before raised a hand to strike her.

Ozeret felt bowed with shame and confusion during that long first week. Each night she lay awake in the uneasy silence of the house listening for clues to the mystery of so much pain.

CHAPTER 8

Ein Karem

One summer morning Elizabeth, dreamily spinning thread in a sunny corner of the room, was surprised to hear steps approaching the house. She rose heavily from her chair and walked to the door.

Elizabeth saw her mother's features and her aunt's and her own in the young woman who stood before her.

Before Elizabeth had time to wonder, Mary seized both of her hands. "My mother has sent me to you," Mary said, "with my mother's servant. We are to stay with you until the autumn rains begin and your baby has arrived. My servant is to help you during your confinement, and I am to grow healthy and strong in the sunlight of your hills."

Elizabeth stared at the pale young woman and was overwhelmed by the time that had passed since she fled Jerusalem with her husband and Judas. She had barely marked time's passage as Judas grew into a young man and she grew old without a child of her own. But now, with her aunt's child standing before her, she felt the full force of all the years she had missed in the city of her childhood with its familiar streets and faces and the Temple that announced the greatness of her people.

Elizabeth stepped away from Mary and put a hand on her own swelling belly. She glanced at the servant standing behind her cousin and recalled the silent girl who had waited upon the family during that long-ago Passover feast. But this woman, her face half hidden in the folds of a black cloak, looked old now too. Again the years Elizabeth had endured like some dumb animal taunted her. Was her own face as lined as the face of her aunt's servant?

Ozeret, Elizabeth remembered suddenly. The servant's name was Ozeret. She would call her that, even though the servant was deaf and mute, because that was the name her aunt had given her. Ozeret had helped her aunt bring Mary into the world, and she would help Elizabeth too.

Elizabeth smelled the flowers and herbs offering themselves up to the warm August sun and to the bees who would return to her hives sated with pollen. Even the three old twisted cypress trees that towered behind the house seemed to be dancing under the cloudless blue sky.

She reached out again for Mary and pulled her as close as her swollen belly allowed. "You remind me of my childhood," she whispered to her cousin. "I welcome you and rejoice to have you here."

MARY OPENED HER eyes to moonlight streaming through a chink in the shuttered window of the tiny bedroom that she had all to herself. Her cousin told her that the shepherd named Judas slept on this pallet when Zachariah's flock came down from the summer pastures. But for now it was hers.

Mary stretched her limbs wide, as far as they would go, arms and legs welcoming the night. For ten years she had woken to the press of girls' bodies and dreams and whispers. And after she returned home, her parents expected her to sleep close to them on the trundle bed her cousin Joseph had built for the purpose.

When Joseph came to welcome her home, he seemed so old, as old as her mother's servant Ozeret. Yet when Mary lay in her trundle bed in her parents' bedroom, pretending to be asleep, she heard her parents whisper their hope that she would soon be Joseph's wife.

Mary envied the servant her mother called Ozeret. She alone had a few hours of privacy each night. And her days were spent in silence. Mary wished she were deaf and mute like Ozeret and could live in her own private world. Maybe then the god of the Temple would speak to her as he spoke to the prophets long ago. The words of the prophets filled her mind and heart making it hard to attend to the voices of the people around her.

But at least for now she had this tiny room and the pallet that belonged to Judas.

As the moonlight moved across the window, Mary remembered her parents' excitement when she first returned home. Her mother led her into the bedroom and helped her change out of her unbleached Temple tunic and put on the finely woven tunic and the blue cloak that were carefully folded at the top of a cedar chest in the bedroom. Mary had never seen such a shade of blue except in the sky above the tiny Temple courtyard where the girls took their exercise. When she walked through the curtain, her old father smiled and tears ran down his wrinkled cheeks catching in his beard.

But before many hours went by on the day she first returned from the Temple, Mary sensed an uneasiness in the house. She felt that her presence ruffled the smooth surface of the day and, later, the intimacy of night.

And now, less than a month after she had come to live with her parents, here she was at the home of her old rabbi. Mary shuddered. But then she recalled the mute old man who huddled in the corner closest to the stove during the day. Ruth had been right. Zachariah had lost the power of speech. And without words, he didn't frighten her.

She shuddered again. An image flashed through her mind. A little girl was dancing under the moon until, into the silence, Zachariah's hand reached out and grabbed her.

The moonlight in Mary's bedroom moved past the chink in the shutters. She pulled herself into a compact ball, impregnable as a hedgehog feigning death, and drifted back to sleep.

When she next awoke the shutters were open and sunlight flooded the room. She could hear her cousin Elizabeth singing in the kitchen.

Mary went to the window. She was amazed by the expanse of the sky and the brightness of the sun and the freedom she felt in the hills beyond the city. Her body felt restless in a way she couldn't understand.

She had been taught by Zachariah that her body was unclean and only useful for increasing the number of the Temple god's chosen people. Her people's god had handed down his laws carved into immutable rock and his priests prescribed every action necessary to keep this god's wrath in check. Mary had struggled to make herself as rigid as the tablets of Moses with the commandments etched into her heart. But life outside the Temple and far from Jerusalem seemed to blur the rules she had learned by rote.

Slowly, as the weeks went by, Mary fell into a new rhythm of peaceful days helping Ozeret with the household tasks and waiting on her cousin. While Elizabeth napped during the long, hot afternoons of summer, Mary took solitary walks in the hills above the village.

Her mother's servant glared her disapproval each time Mary crept from the house while Elizabeth dozed. Mary pretended not to notice. She realized, dimly, that Ozeret was right, that she had no business wandering by herself far from her cousin's home. Yet as soon as the house and village disappeared, Mary felt her spirit lighten and strength fill her. She felt as if she were training for some future time that would require courage beyond her capacity to imagine. So each afternoon she explored the hills for an hour or more, keeping her senses alert for anyone who might see her and report her to her cousin, or, worse still, to her mother in Jerusalem.

One day Elizabeth woke early from her nap and found her cousin gone. When Mary entered the house, bringing with her the scent of herbs and open air, Elizabeth rose heavily from the chair where she sat waiting. "Cousin," she whispered in an anguished voice. "You are to be betrothed to an honorable man in the autumn. How will he marry you if he hears of your wandering the hills alone, not caring what shepherd or traveler might happen upon you and wound you and your family's honor?"

Elizabeth motioned to a chair at the table where Ozeret sat pounding fragrant herbs for the evening's lentil stew. Mary felt the servant's censorious look and glared at her until Ozeret lowered her eyes to the mortar and pestle. And then she listened, her horror deepening, as Elizabeth told her the story of Miriam, the sister of Zachariah and mother of Judas. Mary watched pain etch her cousin's face as she told the story of a young girl, defiled by an unnamed attacker, dying in anguish and leaving a baby for others to raise.

As she sat quietly after the story was over, feeling Elizabeth's hand gently stroking her own, all Mary could think of was Judas and the loneliness of a childhood without a mother's love. She too had such a childhood, although she sometimes remembered, fleetingly, a time before the Temple with a peaceful room and the scent of herbs and the sound of her mother's voice telling stories.

Mary glanced at Ozeret still pounding the herbs, though they must be a fine powder by now. She saw tears in the woman's eyes. Mary was startled. She never before considered that Ozeret might have feelings. Was she noticing the pain on Elizabeth's face, even though she couldn't hear the words? Did she care about Zachariah's long-dead sister, the mother of Judas?

Then Mary wondered what Ozeret knew about her years at home before the Temple. Did Ozeret know when she learned to walk and talk and what foods she ate from her mother's hand after she was weaned? Did this deaf and mute servant witness her parents' tears and imagine their daughter's fear and loneliness during the past ten years?

Mary, keeping her expression calm and her emotions hidden, felt a yearning for her own life before she was handed over to a husband.

As she rose from her chair and knelt beside Elizabeth, with her head in her cousin's lap and murmurs of remorse leaving her mouth to soothe her cousin's ears, Mary resolved to be more careful in the future. She would wait until night to leave the house, making certain that Elizabeth and Zachariah and her mother's servant were sleeping soundly.

Each afternoon, as Elizabeth dozed on her bed behind the curtain, Mary dutifully spun or wove under Ozeret's watchful eye. When Ozeret returned from the spring with the water jug on her head in the late afternoon, Mary woke Elizabeth and helped her to the table for the evening meal. She set Elizabeth's cup of wine before her cousin and smiled as her cousin spoke of swaddling clothes and labor pains and the dreams she had for the baby on its way.

At night, when Zachariah's snores were the only sound inside the house, Mary crept out of her bed and tiptoed past Ozeret. She walked past her aunt's beehives, the bees drowsing inside, and up the path that led to the hillside pastures.

The first time Mary crept away in the night, Ozeret summoned the courage to follow her into the hills.

Mary walked slowly and dreamily, stopping from time to time to pick a white flower that bloomed in the moonlight by the path.

Then Ozeret heard the rustling of sheep. Mary left the path and skirted the hillside, trampling grasses and herbs as she walked. Ozeret kept well behind, following the scent of crushed herbs, until she found herself above the pasture where, in the distance, a shepherd sat in the doorway of a small hut playing his pipes while the sheep grazed below him.

A lamb bleated. The sheep moved frantically up and down the hillside. The shepherd stood up, his red hair gleaming in the moonlight. Ozeret watched the shepherd run after the wolf that held the lamb in its jaws.

When Ozeret's heart stopped pounding, she hurried back to the path. Her legs felt stiff, and the coolness of the dew caused her to shiver inside her cloak.

The walk home seemed to go on and on, as if it were happening in a dream where the laws of time and space were suspended. Finally the house appeared.

Mary stood in the moonlight beside Elizabeth's bee hives staring up into the sky where stars glittered above the looming cypress trees.

Exasperation overcame Ozeret. She started towards the figure of Mary, who was becoming like a shadow as the stars went out and the moon set behind the hill.

Then Ozeret froze.

"I am thy handmaiden," Mary said clearly. "Thy will be done."

Ozeret peered into the darkness beyond Mary, but all she saw was the three cypress trees and the cluster of hives in which hundreds of bees lay resting from their daytime labors.

With her mind darkened by fear and confusion, Ozeret crept into the house and pretended to be sleeping until Mary finally tiptoed through the room.

At first Mary just watched. She sat in the shadows of a cave above the shepherd's hut and watched the sheep graze or doze. The moon was almost full, then full, then waning as she journeyed up the hill each night and sat watching until the dew began to glisten on the grass.

Each night she watched the shepherd appear during the time when the night felt suspended, refusing to move towards the dawn. He appeared when Mary, had she been asleep, would wake in a cold sweat with the pain of a hand wrenching her arm and then darkness and her own sobs lulling her back to sleep.

When he appeared, a small figure below her cave, Mary knew that the night terrors owned him too. She watched and waited to discover what he meant to her.

One night when the moon had waned so much that the shepherd no longer gleamed in the pasture below, Mary found the courage to creep down the hillside.

He turned towards the sound of shifting scree, a shepherd alert for the danger of wolves. Mary called out his name.

Each night she sat with Judas, sometimes just listening to the sounds of nocturnal creatures, sometimes talking quietly, the words not mattering except as they wove a web that trapped them.

Each morning before dawn Mary gathered a leaf of lemon balm that grew beside the path that took her from the pasture to the home of her cousin Elizabeth. All day the leaf infused her cousin's evening cup of wine, ensuring her a restful night of sleep oblivious to Mary's absence.

And so the summer passed, moon waxing and waning, until one early morning Mary crept into the house, smelling of lemon balm and her night under a crescent moon, and was surprised by the sight of her cousin waiting for her just inside the door. But instead of a rebuke, she received her cousin's embrace.

"The baby's kicking woke me," Elizabeth whispered to Mary, "and I left my bed to seek relief in the night air. When I saw you coming down the path, the baby leapt for joy. What miracle is this, Cousin?"

Mary drew apart from her cousin and smiled as she heard the answer deep inside her heart. "My womb shall bring salvation to our people," she answered.

That night, as Elizabeth labored to give birth, Mary felt a humming all around her and heard the beating of thousands of tiny wings. She felt as if she were inside her cousin's hive, the queen of all that was sweetness and life. She moved with dreamy ease, dampening a cloth for her cousin's brow or holding her hand while she screamed. When at last she held the slimy body of a baby boy, while Ozeret cut the cord that bound him to his mother, she heard within her heart, louder than the wings that beat around her, the voice of her god. She listened and nodded her assent.

CHAPTER 9

Jerusalem, one month later

Joseph looked around the Temple courtyard. The space was crowded with young men, descendants of the great King David. These were Mary's suitors, each holding a carved wooden staff gleaming with the oil and prayers his hopeful mother had rubbed into it against a favorable outcome for her son.

Joseph's staff was the finest of them all, intricately carved with a replica of the fig tree and serpentine bench in his garden and the myriad creatures that fluttered and buzzed and burrowed within its walls. The top of the staff was carved into the figure of a lamb whose face seemed to delight in the scene below it.

Joseph had never before carved anything as fine as this. He had barely slept since he started it, shortly after Mary returned from Ein Karem. But his staff lacked a mother's blessing, and he was now too old. So Joseph withdrew his spirit from the scene around him and just hoped to endure the humiliation and disappointment of this day.

Joseph thought about the house, now quiet and peaceful, where he had once endured the taunts and abuse of his father and brothers. Joseph now lived alone in the house, next to his father's workshop, the only one of his father's sons who had not married and fathered children for the House of David. His father's last words, as he lay dying on the bed that Joseph now called his own, were, "Blessings on my married sons and their families who brought me honor in life and a peaceful death."

At night when the streets were quiet and the workshop shuttered and still, Joseph carved intricate animals by the light of his oil lamp and remembered his cousin Mary. His reveries were bittersweet and nostalgic. They had nothing to do with the present or the future. Only the past, when Mary was a child who loved him, mattered to Joseph.

Joseph suddenly recoiled from the thought of his calm, ordered life being shattered by a beautiful young woman he no longer knew.

But then he glanced around at the young men, their faces smooth and their eyes like shallow puddles, and his mind darkened at the thought of their hands touching his cousin Mary or their hearts treating her as if she were just another woman, the one they happened to win.

Then Joseph saw the other suitors nudging one another and murmuring among themselves. He looked where they were staring and saw a tall, thin man, barely out of boyhood, whose red hair and strange blue eyes set him apart as much as his rough shepherd's tunic and simple shepherd's staff.

Could this stranger be Zachariah's nephew? His mother Miriam was of the royal house of David, but he, a bastard whose father, it was rumored, was Zachariah, was an outcast to the people of Israel. Why was Judas here, far from his uncle's flocks, when he should be in the high pasture above his village allowing the sheep to fatten and the lambs to grow strong before the long, cold rains began.

The other men glanced at Judas from time to time and whispered and laughed. Judas didn't seem to notice them. He fixed his blue eyes on the steps leading up to the Temple. Joseph looked in the same direction.

Silence fell as a small procession approached. Mary walked in front, shining in her crimson gown. A blue linen scarf covered her head and shoulders with a becoming modesty, and she looked straight ahead, moving with a grace and authority that belied her fourteen years.

Mary's mother walked behind her, supported by her servant. Ozeret wore the black cloak and hood that hid her face in every kind of weather. Joseph wished that she could speak. He wanted to know about the months in the hills of Judea that had turned Mary into such a self-assured, beautiful woman.

His aunt looked very old and frail. She leaned heavily on the cane Joseph had carved for her after Joachim died.

Joseph still wondered why Anne hadn't sent for Mary and Ozeret to comfort and support her in her grief. Instead she had relied on Joseph to walk with her to the burial cave outside the city walls where she bent to kiss Joachim one last time before her nephews carried him into the cave and rolled the stone across its entrance. Joseph had visited her every day, disheartened by her slatternly servant and the absence of Ozeret's herbs and spices to scent the room and flavor the food. But whenever he offered to send for Mary and Ozeret, his aunt just shook her head.

Mary stopped in front of the head priest.

"Daughter of the House of David," the priest intoned. "These sons of David's lineage await a sign to learn which of them will take you as his wife. Submit to the will of your husband and bring honor to the House of David."

Mary bowed her head in answer. Then she and her mother took their seats opposite the group of suitors to await the outcome.

One by one each suitor stood before the priest with his staff outstretched for blessing. When Joseph's turn arrived, his grizzled head and beard provoked snickers from the young men. They were silenced by a fierce glare from the black-robed priest.

As Joseph stood with downcast eyes, feeling humiliated and old, he heard a voice cry out, "His staff has flowered."

He raised his head and looked at Mary. She was standing up and pointing at his staff. Her cheeks were as crimson as her gown, and her head scarf had slipped to her shoulders. He heard her repeat, "His staff has flowered. His staff has flowered."

Behind him the crowd of suitors buzzed like angry hornets. One of the suitors cursed. The priest drew in his breath, his hands still hovering over Joseph's staff in blessing. Joseph looked down. Mary's voice buzzed, "His staff has flowered. His staff has flowered." The suitors' drone echoed the voice of Mary. "His staff has flowered. His staff has flowered."

Joseph closed his eyes and tried to absent himself from the noise and confusion. He felt dizzy and opened his eyes to get his bearings.

The lamb at the end of his staff, shimmering below the priest's hands, had become a lily.

Joseph blinked his eyes. His lamb was back, but Mary's insistent voice and the roar of the crowd were louder than ever.

A cry of rage and the crack of splintering wood silenced Mary and the suitors. Joseph spun his head around. He watched as Judas, his blue eyes wild with fury, flung his broken staff into the crowd of disappointed suitors.

Joseph turned to look at Mary. He waited until she turned her gaze from Judas and smiled serenely at him. Then he took her arm and led her before the priest to receive his blessing on their betrothal.

JUDAS RUSHED THROUGH the Temple courtyards until he reached the sweeping marble steps that led to the busy shops and crowded street below. He ran, stumbling and cursing, down the steps and then stood panting and shaking with rage.

Judas remembered the words Mary had spoken to him after their last night in his uncle's pasture.

"My womb is blessed, Judas. Shalom."

The next night Judas waited for Mary, but she never came to him. So Judas gathered up his uncle's flock and led them down the hill to his uncle's sheepfold.

When he came to his uncle's house, he heard an infant crying. A girl from the village, her bare feet coated with dust and grime, was setting the table for the midday meal. Through the bedroom curtain Judas saw Elizabeth and the wailing baby. Elizabeth looked haggard and old, but she smiled a greeting to Judas.

There was no blue cloak hanging from a peg. There was no pallet in the corner for Ozeret.

"This baby's name is John," Elizabeth told him. "His birth has returned your uncle to himself. Zachariah speaks again and has gone to Jerusalem with my cousin Mary to make a worthy sacrifice for so much joy and to witness her betrothal."

His aunt continued talking as Judas, horrified, watched her mouth move.

"Mary will sacrifice doves for me in the Temple to give thanks for this great blessing."

The baby's shrill crying intensified as Judas fled from the house and village. He found himself, hours later, standing at the gate to Jerusalem.

JUDAS FELT A hand tighten around his wrist. He shook his arm savagely trying to get free. The grip tightened.

At first Judas struggled. He cursed the man with every insult he knew. He cursed Joseph for taking Mary from him. He cursed Zachariah and the priests of the Temple and, finally, he cursed the god of his people who had betrayed him once again. The man beside him seemed indifferent to the invective that turned, finally, into shaking sobs. He pulled and dragged Judas through the streets and through the city gate and up the hill towards the Mount of Olives.

At last they stopped, half way up the Mount of Olives, and rested in front of a cave. Judas gazed down the hill at the Temple gleaming under the clear blue autumn sky. His mind cleared and he wiped his face on the sleeve of his mantle.

The man took bread and a flask of wine from a pouch beneath his mantle and offered them to Judas. Judas ripped off a piece of bread and drank deeply from the flask. Then the man began to speak.

"We sit before the cave of Nicodemus" he said, "a young man of noble birth whose ancestors lie buried here. He awaits salvation for our people."

At the word "salvation" all Judas's pain and anger returned; he struggled to get up and flee. But the man reached out his strong arm and restrained him.

"Salvation means many things," the man continued, as calmly as if Judas had not struggled and spat and cursed before settling down once again. "For the woman Joseph the Carpenter won today, salvation is a husband and a family to enrich the people of Israel."

Judas started to struggle again, and again the man restrained him.

"And she is right. Each woman must bear fruit until, one day, our messiah will be born to us. But I grow impatient. I cannot wait for a baby to become a man and lead us into battle with our Roman oppressors."

For the first time the man's voice became agitated. Judas glanced at him uneasily.

"I find," the man said angrily, rising to his feet, "that my salvation can only come each time I slay a Roman soldier. Perhaps one day I'll kill the man who raped my wife and murdered our unborn child."

The man regained his composure as quickly as he lost it.

"I seek more men to join me in fighting our oppressors and hastening the day of our salvation. Will you find your own salvation by joining me?"

As the man spoke, Judas remembered the Roman soldiers who stole crops from the terraced plots beyond Ein Karem, leaving the people of the village to struggle and starve through the long, rainy months of winter. He pictured the tax collector who exacted tribute money for the Roman emperor each year from families who could ill afford the half shekel already owed to the Temple. Every memory of a clean-shaven face incited in Judas a fierce desire for revenge.

For the first time Judas looked closely at his companion. The man stood calmly under the scrutiny. Judas saw that the man was short and stocky. He appeared to be in his late twenties, still vigorous but with deep lines etched between his nose and the corners of his mouth and a complex cross hatching of wrinkles in the corners of his eyes. His beard and hair were coarse and wiry and beginning to gray. He was balding; his head glistened with sweat, whether from the rapid climb or suppressed emotion Judas could only guess. Judas felt darkness roiling inside the man, the same darkness that haunted his own mind and peace. This man, like Judas, had lost everything. And yet he still had a plan and a direction for his life.

"Ah," the man said. "You are considering my words. We need men like you, bent but not broken, to fight for our people. My name is Seth. I welcome you to your new life."

Judas followed Seth back into the city and down the winding streets far from the Temple and the homes of wealthy priests and government officials. When they arrived at the meanest section of the city, a maze of stinking alleys on the outskirts of King Herod's grandiose urban renewal, Seth led Judas into a small, dark room where two boys sat at a table eating lentil stew and talking quietly.

Seth motioned Judas to the only remaining chair and stood leaning against the door. He began speaking to the boys as if continuing a conversation that had been interrupted.

"In a few months the streets of Bethlehem will be full of men forced to leave their families in the cold of winter to travel to the City of David for the Roman census. Tempers will be tinder dry and ready to flare. We now have the man to lead you."

Judas looked around but saw only the two boys and Seth.

"Judas is of royal blood and ready to seek salvation," Seth said. "He hides as a simple shepherd. With him to lead you, you can slip into the city and start the conflagration that will consume our oppressors and disrupt the emperor's attempt to count us as if we were bags of grain in his storehouses. From this day on you will follow Judas with courage and rage and return to me when you can."

Seth handed Judas a heavy purse.

"These coins are from our patron Nicodemus," Seth told him. "Use them to buy whatever you need."

Seth turned to the young boys who were looking respectfully at Judas. "Tomorrow you will show Judas the cave above Bethlehem where you can watch the city and plan your disruption."

Judas stared incredulously at Seth. Then he shrugged and tucked the purse inside his tunic.

The meal Ozeret had prepared grew cold, the lentils congealing in the pot. Mary's words, spoken before she and her mother had begun to eat, repeated themselves in Ozeret's head until she felt as if she would explode from her anger at Mary and her own guilt for not preventing this tragedy.

"Mother, I am pregnant. God's spirit has sanctified my womb. Joseph, my betrothed, must allow me to live with him as his virgin bride and raise the son I carry."

Ozeret pondered Mary's words, her anger turning into grudging admiration tinged with fear. Where did this young woman, just a few months out of the Temple compound, get such ruthless imagination and power? How did she manage to make the priest and the suitors, and maybe even herself, believe that a miracle occurred, turning the wooden lamb on Joseph's staff into a lily? She had to marry Joseph. Who else would accept a pregnant bride? But how had she made everyone believe in a miracle that never happened? Was it because she herself believed that a wooden lamb could become a lily if that's what the voice she heard required? Ozeret shivered. Perhaps Mary even believed that spirit impregnated her, not the shepherd Judas. Perhaps she convinced her cousin Elizabeth as well.

Ozeret needed to touch something real. She sidled past the table to her pallet and took up her spindle. Keeping her eyes on the thread, she heard her mistress finally respond to Mary in a voice so cold Ozeret imagined the tears had frozen on her cheeks.

"Daughter, spirit gives each human creature the divine spark that raises it above the beasts. But each human body requires the seed of man to make it grow. Your womb should have awaited Joseph to bring it to life. Its quickening now brings shame to me and to the memory of your father."

Ozeret heard the scraping of a chair and the sound of the curtain being drawn across her mistress's bedroom. Then she heard Mary's footsteps and felt a hand touch her lightly on the shoulder.

Reluctantly, Ozeret looked up from her spinning. Mary, wrapped in her blue cloak, pointed to the door.

Ozeret's heart filled with dismay at the prospect of leaving her mistress alone, but she bowed her submission to Mary and set aside her spinning. Then she took her black cape from the foot of her pallet and followed Mary through the narrow streets until they came to Joseph's shop.

Ozeret stood behind Mary in the open doorway. Joseph had exchanged his formal robe for a simple tunic and leather apron and was bent over a small, round table which he was sanding. He stopped to run his hand over the surface, testing its smoothness.

Through the open shutter of a window on the far side of the workshop Ozeret could glimpse the courtyard with its fig tree, stripped of fruit but still leafy green, and the serpentine bench that wound around it. She tried to imagine Mary's child playing in that garden.

Joseph looked up from his work and saw his future wife standing in the entrance to his shop. Ozeret saw the look of confusion on his face.

"Cousin, may I speak with you?" Mary asked calmly.

Slowly Joseph nodded his grizzled head. "Shall we go to the house?" he asked.

Ozeret saw Mary look through the open windows into the garden beyond. "May we speak in the garden?"

Joseph opened the door beside the open window and led her into the garden, fragrant with herbs basking in the autumn sunlight. Ozeret breathed deeply of the rosemary and mints and thyme and felt the ordered peace of this place calm her spirit. She stood by the western wall of the garden, where Joseph had carved the top of a post into an energetic little lamb with its laughing head upturned to the sky, and watched Mary and Joseph from deep within the dark folds of her cloak.

Joseph motioned Mary to the serpentine bench that wound around the fig tree and then sat stiffly beside her, staring straight ahead, with his large, rough hands clasped awkwardly in his lap. Ozeret watched

Mary place her small hand on Joseph's arm and wait until he turned his face to her.

Ozeret plucked a sprig of rosemary and rubbed it almost violently between her fingers. She watched Joseph's face go gray and his shoulders slump as Mary said, "Cousin, we must marry right away. I am with child."

Ozeret ached for Joseph and wondered what he would say to the confident young woman who had so calmly shattered his world.

Joseph was silent for so long that Ozeret began to notice the sounds in the garden. Bees buzzed and butterflies flapped their wings. A fly landed on the carved lamb's head, and a mosquito whirred by Ozeret's ear. She was so engrossed in all this activity that she almost missed the sound of Joseph's voice, thick with misery, as he answered Mary.

"Mary, I have loved you since your birth and your mother as if she were my own. But how can I accept this shame to me and to our family? Why did you wait until we were betrothed in the Temple, before our god and our people, to tell me of your disgrace?"

Mary rose from the bench and stood facing Joseph. Ozeret saw her smile at him and wait quietly, her face so lovely beneath her blue scarf. Finally Joseph spoke in a voice so low and trembling that Ozeret could barely make it out. "You leave me no choice," he whispered. "I have always loved you and love you still. Thy will be done." Then he rose and offered her his arm.

Ozeret followed them back into the workshop and out into the street. There Mary nodded to Joseph and walked back towards her mother's house. Ozeret paused to look at Joseph and was appalled by the misery she saw in his face. She lowered her head and hurried after Mary.

OZERET FELT COLDER than she could ever remember. Each night she huddled under her woolen blanket, now so thin in spots that she could see her hand through it. She felt as lonely and abandoned as the little girl she used to be when she spent her nights terrorized by the men and rats of the city streets, who, with the feral cats, were her only companions.

The silence in the house unnerved her as much as the skittering and footfalls in the streets of her childhood. Why did Mary lie behind her bedroom curtain, never speaking, always keeping her stories and her dreams from Joseph? Why didn't Joseph reach for his bride and fill the house with the sounds and smells of their love?

Ozeret wondered what Mary felt when she first saw her mother lying pale and still, her slight and withered body barely disturbing the bed covers. Did she feel remorse for shaming her mother into such despair that her spirit left her?

On the very afternoon that her mother was placed beside her father in the burial cave outside the walls of the city, Mary sent Joseph to fetch the trunk that held her father's scrolls and the cabinet that held her mother's spices and bring them to her new home.

Sometimes during the day, while Joseph was busy in his workshop and Mary sat quietly reading her father's scrolls, the familiar smell of ink and parchment helped Ozeret pretend that she was back in the home of her first mistress. She could imagine that Joachim was at the Temple and that Mary, her belly swelling beneath her tunic, was her first mistress, made joyful by conceiving after so many barren years.

But then the silence would close in on Ozeret, and she missed the sounds that came from her first mistress's mouth as her eyes moved across the marks on the parchment. When Mary read, the thin line of her mouth stayed as tightly closed as the door of her mother's spice cabinet.

One of Ozeret's few pleasures in this new life was opening the cabinet door with the key she had been entrusted with years before. The key hung on a piece of leather around her neck. It rested between her breasts and comforted her with its smooth, unchanging surface kept warm by her own flesh. When Ozeret pulled the key from her tunic and unlocked the cabinet door, she existed for a timeless moment in the complex mix of smells that suspended her above and beyond her present cares.

Sometimes Ozeret wondered if such riches were hidden within Mary. She moved so gracefully, despite her growing belly, and her face always showed the same untroubled beauty. But Mary never opened so much as a tiny crack. Whatever treasures lay hidden behind the smooth brow and cheeks that curved so like her mother's remained as much a mystery as the life that grew within her womb.

OZERET PACKED FOOD and a change of linens for Joseph's journey to Bethlehem. It would take him the better part of the day to walk over the hills from Jerusalem to the city of King David. He would be lucky to arrive before dark.

Ozeret had heard mutterings and complaints in the streets about the Roman census. With the cold and rains of winter upon them and the taxes and tithes of empire and Temple emptying their purses, the people of Jerusalem were already worn down and discouraged. Now every head of a household must return to the city of his family's origin to be counted for the Roman census.

Ozeret worried about Joseph. He looked so frail, and she wondered if he still had kin in Bethlehem. Where would he spend the night after his journey? She touched his shoulder gently as she moved around the table serving the evening meal. She wished she could tell him that she would care for Mary in his absence. Instead she pictured his pregnant wife safe and warm by the fire awaiting his return and hoped he could see what she was imagining.

Mary seemed unperturbed. After supper Ozeret heard her rustling about behind the bedroom curtain while Joseph attended to some matter in his workshop. Then Mary came back into the room and unrolled a scroll on the table Ozeret had wiped and polished. The sweet odor of the olive oil lamp filled the room.

Ozeret polished the plates and goblets and put them on the intricately carved shelf Joseph had built. She rubbed her own bowl clean with a scrap of bread and then ran her finger along its familiar crack before putting the bowl on the floor by the water jug. Then she ate the bread and went to her pallet to spin thread and wait for her master and mistress to end this day.

Finally Mary rolled up the scroll and went behind the curtain to put it back in its chest. Ozeret heard Joseph, who had long since gone to bed, grumble when Mary lifted the lid of the chest.

When Mary reentered the room, she signaled to Ozeret that she was ready to retire.

Ozeret tiptoed into the bed chamber to fetch Mary's night shift and comb. Joseph's slight body was huddled under the blankets. Ozeret could feel his restless misery.

Ozeret helped her mistress into the woolen shift she wore during winter nights and then led her to a chair by the stove. Mary sat quietly while Ozeret unbraided and combed her long, fine hair and then twisted it into a knot and bound it in a linen head scarf.

Ozeret was confounded each night when her mistress entered the bed chamber with her hair as hidden from her husband as it was from the rest of the world during the day. She wished for Joseph that he could see how Mary's hair danced in the lamp light before Ozeret hid it in the shadows of a head scarf. She wished even more that he could stroke its silky softness as Ozeret did each night when she prepared her mistress for sleep.

Ozeret knew that Joseph loved beauty, especially to touch it with his long, supple fingers. She watched him whenever he neglected to close the door to his workshop. He tested the wood he was turning or sanding by the caress of his hand more than with his eyes. Sometimes Ozeret allowed herself to imagine the feel of those hands, and she wondered why Mary seemed to recoil from her husband's touch.

Ozeret returned the chair to its place at the table and banked the fire. Then she put on her cloak and hurried to the nearby alley where she squatted in the shadows. When she returned to the house, all was quiet. Ozeret spread her cloak over the threadbare blanket and settled herself for sleep. First she stroked a strand of her hair, now coarse where gray streaked it but always a reminder, before she slept, of her existence in a world that rarely saw her. Then she clasped the key around her neck and murmured the blessing her old master spoke in her first home. The memory of those words and the scent of the spice cabinet kept her company through the long night.

OZERET WAS SHOCKED out of sleep during the cold and dark of the early winter morning. Joseph's voice was raised in anger. Ozeret had never heard that sound before.

Mary's voice, calm and sure, replied to his outrage. "I shall go with you to Bethlehem. It is written on my father's scroll that my child will be born in King David's city."

Joseph and Mary emerged from behind their curtain. Mary said, "The servant will prepare a meal to break our fast. Here are my clothes and the swaddling clothes for the child. Prepare your donkey for our journey."

Joseph walked to his workshop, leaving the door open. Ozeret watched him get the donkey's panniers from their hook and the blanket from its rack. Then, without putting on a cloak against the frigid air, he left his workshop to feed and load the donkey. When he returned, he was shivering from the cold. His cheeks looked hollow and his shoulders sagged. Mary looked up from her plate and smiled serenely.

While Mary used the chamber pot behind the curtain, Joseph filled the donkey's panniers with food and clothing and the baby's swaddling clothes. Ozeret knew the journey would take much longer with the burden of a laden donkey and frequent stops for Mary. She silently lamented that she would be expected to take part in this strange procession instead of staying home near the fire ready to fetch the midwife. But she went about her duties, emptying the chamber pot into the gutter, handing bedrolls and food and linens to Joseph when he led the donkey to the door, fastening the blue woolen cape around her mistress's shoulders and tying the hood under her chin, stirring the ashes of the fire to make sure the embers were dead, and then, finally, putting on her own thin black cloak. She helped Joseph lift Mary, bulky and clumsy and grimacing with pain, onto the small donkey. The little beast sagged under the unaccustomed weight. Joseph locked the heavy wooden door and hung the key around his neck. Ozeret handed him the donkey's reins and then followed Mary, Joseph, and the unborn baby through the streets that crunched with frost underfoot, wondering what awaited them in the town of Bethlehem.

CHAPTER 10

Bethlehem

The sky was a threadbare black cloak barely covering the light that twinkled through its many rips and tears and making midnight on the hillside as bright as noon. Judas huddled inside the cave he had discovered the week before. It was hidden from the path that led to Bethlehem.

The lamb he had found just after sunset lay still and cold in his lap. What ewe would be so careless as to birth a lamb in winter he thought angrily as he stroked the tiny, lifeless body.

Judas carried the lamb out into the brilliant night and walked until he found an overhanging rock. He tucked the stiff body as far under the rock as he could and returned to the cave.

Reuben and Aaron were waiting for him. They grew silent as he approached. Sometimes Judas wondered why jokes and banter faded as soon as he arrived. But tonight he was still thinking about the senseless death of the lamb and barely noticed that they were there.

Judas settled himself on his bedroll and stared moodily through the cave's entrance not seeing the starry hillside outside the gloom of the cave and his own dark thoughts. He felt his mind fill with the task at hand.

Always it was revenge. Revenge lifted the darkness that had smothered him for as long as he could remember. Revenge eased the pain of losing Mary. Revenge gave him a power and purpose that he had never known before.

Until he left Ein Karem, following Mary and her servant to Jerusalem, he had not known that there were other men who wanted to lash out against the world.

Aaron's voice outside the cave startled Judas. He went outside. "What star is that?" Aaron asked above the steady stream of his piss.

Judas looked up and was shocked by an unfamiliar brightness where no star had ever been. Although he could name every constellation in the winter sky and was as familiar with their stars as with the rocks along the path from Ein Karem to his uncle's pasture, he had no name for the enormous star that illuminated the town of Bethlehem. He shrugged, trying to hide his astonishment from the boy.

When they returned to the cave, Reuben was snoring loudly. The closeness of the space reeking of sweat and sheep made Judas eager to be out in the bright, sweet-smelling night. He shook Reuben awake.

Reuben grumbled as he sat up and rubbed his eyes. Then he noticed the brilliance of the starlight as it illuminated the cave's entrance and hurried to his feet.

Silently they gathered up their bedrolls and, all need for sleep forgotten, followed the star down the hill to Bethlehem.

By the time Joseph led the exhausted donkey into Bethlehem, night had fallen. The town was illuminated by the most brilliant star Joseph had ever seen. The unusual light kept people out in the streets, and the town had a festive feeling that belied the reason it was so full of visitors. Even the Roman soldiers seemed affected by the radiance of the sky and ignored the curfew they were supposed to enforce at sundown. Joseph could barely navigate the donkey through the crowded streets as he sought shelter for the night.

Finally, after an hour or more of knocking at doors and asking anyone who would stop and listen, Joseph stood paralyzed with exhaustion and despair. A soldier jostled Ozeret as she tried to steady Mary on the donkey. Joseph recalled himself and tugged the donkey's reins.

Soon the street became rougher and narrowed, quickly turning into a footpath that headed back up into the hills. The last sign of habitation was a rough stone hut with a wooden shed attached to one wall. Joseph stopped in front of the hut's wooden door and knocked.

The hut was silent and dark. Joseph feared that its inhabitants were out in the streets. Then he heard a shuffling sound and a tiny, bent old woman peered out into the starry street. Her eyes darted to Mary slumped over her huge belly and back to Joseph. She put a gnarled finger to her lips and gestured towards the shed. Then she tugged on Joseph's cloak until he lowered his head. She whispered something in his ear. Joseph nodded his assent and smiled his gratitude. Then the woman scurried back into the house with surprising speed and pulled the door closed behind her.

Joseph walked over to Mary and took her face in his hands. Her eyes were drooping, and her skin felt clammy. "We will stay in the shed this night," he said. "The man in the house won't abide us."

Mary's eyes widened with fear and pain. Joseph held her gaze. Then he spoke in a voice that sounded equal parts anger and compassion. "Thy will be done, Mary," he said. "We are in the city where you say your child must be born. And we have arrived at the only place that will have us."

Ozeret helped Joseph lower Mary from the donkey. She took off her black cloak and spread it on the pile of straw that Joseph had raked into a corner. The sheep droppings were easy for Joseph to scoop up, and he had removed any straw that reeked of urine. Shivering in the damp cold of the stall they were sharing with a ewe and her lamb, as well as their own exhausted donkey, Ozeret settled her mistress on the straw.

Mary's face shone with a waxy pallor, and her forehead gleamed with sweat despite the cold. Joseph watched Ozeret finger the pouch of herbs that hung around her neck on the same piece of leather as the key to the spice cabinet. Without fire, she had no way to brew a tea to ease Mary's pain and hasten her labor. Joseph caught Ozeret's eye and shook his head in commiseration. Then he settled himself in the corner of the stall where the ewe stood nursing her lamb and felt himself slip into sleep.

Before he saw the little stone hut and the ramshackle shed on the outskirts of Bethlehem, Judas heard the cry. He remembered the sound that led him to the dying lamb a few hours before, but he realized this was the cry of a human baby. He quickened his pace and heard Aaron and Reuben quicken theirs a few steps behind him.

Around a curve in the path the town appeared, its stone houses glittering and gleaming under the brilliant night sky. Judas hurried down the hillside to the source of the sound. He stopped at the shed and looked over the half wall that separated it from the street.

The shed was full of shadows, but the starlit street gave some light. Judas heard the rustling of straw and made out the form of a ewe with a lamb tottering on spindly legs and tugging at a teat. Behind her he saw a small donkey with its head lowered in sleep. Judas's eyes, growing used to the dim interior of the shed, made out some people on a pile of straw that leaned against the stone wall of the hut. He saw a man's bald head bent over, unprotected by the hood of his cloak, and the white head of someone who was curled up against the cold without any cloak at all. Between these two figures a woman sat wrapped in a blue robe. She bent over her breast. Starlight fell through a chink in the roof and circled the tiny, downy head of the nursing infant.

Mary looked up. He met her eyes. Then his knees buckled and darkness overcame him. He knew nothing more until he found himself back in the hills with the brothers' anxious faces staring down at him.

Ozeret's dreams were full of cold and dread and the face of a shepherd whose mad blue eyes stared at her while the lamb he held bleated miserably. Each time she woke from this nightmare, she saw

Mary with the infant at her breast and told herself that all was well. But each time she dozed again, the shepherd and the lamb returned. Finally she tired of the nightmare and rose stiffly to relieve herself in the corner of the stall behind the donkey. She stood for a moment warming herself at the donkey's side. Then the infant began to cry.

Joseph sat up and pulled his hood over his head. He looked around him in confusion, as if some dream that still held him were more real than this shadowy, cold shed reeking of urine and excrement and bloody hours of childbirth. Ozeret walked over to him and laid her hand on his shoulder. Then she went to Mary.

Mary's labor had been short but violent, and her screams had brought a man, hairy and dark and with a crude, leering face, out to the stall where he watched Mary's agony for a few minutes and then returned, grumbling and complaining, to the hovel next door. Ozeret winced when she heard the thud and the cry through the unchinked stone wall. She imagined the tiny form of the old woman lying on the dirt floor. But then Mary squeezed her hand so hard that the bones cracked and uttered a cry that covered the violence on the other side of the wall.

Through the coldest hours of the bright-lit night Mary sweated and writhed the new life from her womb and finally, before the pale light of dawn extinguished the stars, the baby fought his way into the stench and chill of the stable. Ozeret suspended him by his tiny feet above Mary's belly and slapped his slippery bottom. His cry woke Joseph. Ozeret nodded at the pouch by his side where he carried his knife. Joseph stared at her without comprehension while the baby wailed in the cold.

Mary's voice rose above the baby's cries. "Joseph, give the servant your knife. She must cut the cord and swaddle the child."

Slowly Joseph moved his hand to the pouch and took out his knife. The blade gleamed in the starlight that filtered through the roof. Ozeret took the handle of the knife from Joseph's outstretched hand. She felt the intricate serpent Joseph had carved into the olivewood. It provided a steady grip as she cut the cord. Then she wiped the blade on her tunic and handed the knife back to him.

Despite her cold and exhaustion and the residue of night terrors that had tormented her brief rest, Ozeret felt a sympathetic smile tug at her mouth when she saw that Joseph had closed his eyes against the sight of his knife and the infant's cord. She laid the baby on his mother's belly and walked over to Joseph. She took his hand and placed the handle in it. When he opened his eyes, she smiled at him. Her heart ached for the confusion in his eyes and the pallor of his face.

Ozeret fetched a bundle of linens from one of the panniers that hung over the stable's half wall. She put the bundle on clean straw and took out a linen cloth. After cleaning the baby as well as she could with a corner of the linen dipped into the ewe's water bucket, she dried him off as he wailed against the cold. Then she wrapped him in the swaddling clothes Mary had packed and handed him back to his mother.

Ozeret watched as the baby nursed and Mary's womb expelled the placenta. When Ozeret was satisfied that Mary's womb was empty, she dried her legs and shrunken belly and pulled down her woolen tunic. She wrapped Mary's blue cape tightly around her. Ozeret's black cape, spread beneath Mary, felt wet, but Ozeret didn't want to risk moving the new mother. She signaled to Joseph to remove his cape. He handed it to her, and she spread it over Mary and the child. Then she found the rake in a corner of the shed and scooped up as much of the bloody straw as she could without disturbing the dozing mother. The infant's eyes were open and seemed to follow her movements whenever she came near, though she knew he was too young to be able to see. She smiled at him in sympathy. They were both powerless in this world. Ozeret felt her heart warm with a love she hadn't felt since the death of her first mistress.

Joseph opened the stable door for Ozeret, and she carried the bloody bundle of straw up the path and into the hills until she found an overhanging rock with a deep crevice. She knelt down and pushed the straw as far into the crevice as it would go. Then, as sunrise colored the hills, Ozeret breathed her thanks for the birth of this grandson of her first mistress and a supplication to the rising sun and the winter-brown hills for his safe passage through this world.

When she stood up, Ozeret was so cold she couldn't feel her fingers or her toes. She walked stiffly down the path to the stable hugging her arms to her chest and emptying her mind of any thought but the command to lift one foot and then the other until she returned to her mistress and the duties of this new day.

Women stood in doorways selling food to the visitors, lentils heaped on unleavened bread, olives, and sticky pieces of honeycomb to sweeten sour wine. The narrow alleys off the main streets that led to the central marketplace added the stench of refuse and human waste to the smells of food and unwashed bodies.

Ozeret rested for a moment in an empty doorway. She longed for Joseph's peaceful garden with its fig tree and fragrant herbs and the smell of sawdust and oiled wood from the workshop if the door into the garden was ajar. She longed for the order of his home and the mystery behind the door of the spice cabinet, the smells that always took her to a peaceful place outside time and pain.

Ozeret felt panicky and hungry and unclean. She balanced the empty water jug on her head and tried to catch someone's attention for directions to the well, but the throng of mostly men ignored her mute signals. Then she caught a glimpse of a familiar head taller than the other men's. Judas's auburn hair gleamed in the sun. Ozeret pushed her way towards him, losing sight of him and then catching a glimpse again.

Judas was leaning against a wall breaking his fast. His eyes looked wild and red rimmed as they darted around the marketplace.

Ozeret stood in front of him and tugged on the sleeve of his cloak. She pointed to the jug on her head beseechingly. Judas fixed his disconcerting eyes on her and then muttered something to one of his companions, a boy much shorter than he who looked to be very much afraid. Then Judas cleared a path through the crowd for Ozeret, shoving people out of the way with a roughness that made her feel mortified and uneasy.

Soon they arrived at a smaller square near the edge of Bethlehem, and Ozeret was relieved to see the familiar scene of women and older girls waiting patiently, their jugs on their heads, as they jostled and joked in line or called out to the younger children who raced around the line and the well or sat playing with pebbles or shards of pottery.

The confusion in the center of Bethlehem, full of soldiers and angry visitors and townspeople hustling food and homemade wares, was muted by the twisting streets and crowded buildings. Ozeret felt the return of peace in her heart as she filled the jug with water and knew that she could soon cleanse her mistress and the baby and then herself from the ordeal of the night.

Judas waited for Ozeret as she filled the jug. The women and children stared at him. He looked wild with his flaming hair and red-rimmed blue eyes and agitated body. And he was a man. A man had no place near the well waiting for a servant to fill her family's jug. Ozeret could hear the women whispering about Judas and about her and was eager to leave, even if it meant traveling through the chaos of the crowded marketplace again and being jostled by angry men and strutting soldiers. She walked quickly back the way they had come, nodding her thanks to Judas and hoping that he would pass her and return to his companions.

To her surprise, Judas put his hand on her arm and stopped her. They leaned against the wall of a house as two women hurried by with their jugs on their heads. The women were so caught up in talk and laughter that they took no notice of the strange couple waiting for them to pass. Then Judas spoke urgently to Ozeret. "Does Mary need food?" he asked. "Are she and the baby safe?"

Ozeret felt the jug on her head totter. She put up her other hand to steady it then looked at Judas.

He had spoken to her. He knew that she could hear and understand. His face was haggard and his blue eyes glittering and almost mad. But his voice when he spoke to her was gentle and sane.

"I watched you, Ozeret, in my uncle's house. Do you remember that evening when I brought more wool for my aunt to spin and then stayed on for supper?"

Ozeret nodded slightly, steadying the jug as her eyes again looked into Judas's. She remembered that evening very well for it had been the next afternoon that Mary had begun her practice of wandering alone in the hills.

Ozeret had believed herself to be invisible as usual as she sat in her corner, missing her mistress in Jerusalem and wondering how long Mary's visit with her cousin was meant to be. Would they stay until Elizabeth gave birth? That must be still three more moons. Ozeret dreaded being separated from her mistress for that long.

Ozeret heard Judas's voice rising and felt his hand on her shoulder. She pulled herself back to the present. "A boy?" she heard Judas ask. Ozeret nodded. "And Mary is well?" Again she nodded yes.

Judas reached inside his tunic and handed Ozeret something wrapped in a scrap of linen. The object was small and heavy for its size. "Please keep this for my son."

Ozeret looked up at Judas. Then she unwrapped the object and stared at the smooth piece of obsidian in her hand. Etched into its gleaming black surface was the outline of a scorpion.

THE STREETS WERE crowded with men eager to register with the census takers and then linger at the marketplace taking in the novelty of different sights and faces. Already a long line stretched around the square and backed up into the street. Three officials behind a long table were ponderously entering the names of the heads of household who waited, with growing impatience, for their turn. Judas watched the crowd carefully, trying to decide how long it would take for this impatience to tip into violence.

One of the three census takers got up and disappeared into the building behind the table. Judas listened to men muttering to each other as the morning wore on and the third census taker failed to return. Here and there among the men were women and children, and the fussing of the children and complaining of the women added to the restless energy in the square.

Judas nodded in the direction of a street beside the census takers' table. Reuben and Aaron followed him, past the Roman soldiers who were moving through the crowd in groups of two and three, leaving ripples of anger in their wake.

They walked up the street away from the marketplace and then ducked into an alley between two houses. The alley reeked of urine and rotting garbage. Judas felt the bile rise in his throat and felt a sudden longing for the clean, soft air of his uncle's pasture.

Judas looked from Reuben to Aaron. "Are you ready?" he asked.

The brothers nodded. They looked too frightened to speak.

"The crowd is getting restless," Judas said. "When they see us act against the soldiers, they'll want to join in."

Judas led Aaron and Reuben to a shed at the end of the alley. He scrambled up to its roof with the other two following him.

Then they made their way, roof by roof, back to the marketplace.

The sun was high overhead by the time they crouched and crawled to the roof of the building behind the census takers. At a signal from Judas, they stood up and aimed their slingshots at three soldiers guarding the table. Aaron and Reuben's missiles found their targets, and two of the soldiers fell to the ground. Judas's rock whizzed by the third soldier and struck an old man squarely on the temple. Judas watched the old man collapse against the third soldier. Then Aaron tugged at his arm, and they ran across the rooftops away from the tumult in the square.

Judas posted Aaron to watch the riot in the marketplace while he and Reuben guarded the street that led to the stable where Mary and the baby lay. When Aaron reported that the brief insurrection had been quelled, Judas ordered the disheartened boys back to Jerusalem without him.

They pleaded with him. Seth's orders were firm and his temper, when crossed, could be frightening. But Judas was implacable. He scratched a note to their leader on a writing slat he produced from his tunic and handed it to Aaron. Aaron read it dubiously. He started to argue with Judas. Seth hadn't authorized Judas to stay in Bethlehem doing reconnaissance. But the look on Judas's face must have been more frightening than their fear of Seth's future reprimand. So the boys hurried out of the city, past the stable where Judas's son lay, and into the hills.

After the crowds in Bethlehem dispersed to the villages of Judea or back to Jerusalem, a few still limping from the skirmish in the square, Judas watched Joseph settle Mary and his son into an inn that now had a room for them. The next day the family, followed by Ozeret, left the inn. Judas darted from alley to alley watching as his son was carried to Bethlehem's synagogue to be circumcised. Judas saw that Mary looked very pale. His son was just a bundle of swaddling clothes and blanket in her arms. But when a cry rang out through the walls of the synagogue reaching Judas where he huddled in an alley, Judas rejoiced to hear the force of his son's lungs and to know that the rabbi's knife and prayers had made his son a child of the god of Israel.

Judas crept from Bethlehem and sat in the shelter of a rock to think about his son. As he rested, a strange caravan approached the little town from the direction of Jerusalem.

The first camel was led by a boy of ten or so. His skin was as black as a night with neither moon nor stars, and a blue and white striped piece of cloth was wrapped around his head. Two more camels followed.

Three men sat perched high on chairs fastened between the camels' humps. The men looked straight ahead as if into a world quite different from the winter-deadened hills of Judea, brightened only by the patchy green of herbs. Their robes of scarlet and vermillion and a blue so deep it seemed to take all the color from the sky brightened the hills and lifted Judas's spirits.

Behind the camels marched a small army of boys carrying trunks and baskets and bundles of every size and shape. Judas huddled at the side of the path feeling his eyes widen to take it all in and breathing in scents so complex and exotic, mingled with the unfamiliar stench of the camels, that he forgot where he was. He watched the procession twist down the hillside and past the first houses of Bethlehem. Then he stood up and followed the wonder of sight and smell until the procession stopped in front of the inn where Mary and the baby rested.

One servant unstrapped a stool from his back and helped each man dismount from each kneeling camel. Then the astonished inn keeper led the three men into his house while the camels and servants waited, completely blocking the narrow street.

Soon a crowd gathered in every alley and on every roof top. Judas was jostled far from the inn and had to wait impatiently for an hour or more until the people made way for the camels and their strange passengers and servants to leave the town for whatever mysterious place next beckoned.

Ozeret stood in a corner of the room in the inn and watched and listened to the three men in their dusty, sumptuous silk robes that smelled of spitting camels and exotic servants and the scent of far off, mysterious places. They had hailed Mary as the god bearer. She nodded serenely. Then each knelt before the baby and hailed him as the messiah their stars foretold.

The most restless of the three first told of their visit with Herod. A star that streaked across the sky led them to his palace, but when they tried to explain what their books and the skies foretold, Herod's manner made them uneasy. He seemed to recoil from the joyous news that the messiah was born at last and that they sought him to pay him homage.

The tallest man took up the tale with the brief observation that Herod was but half a child of Israel; the other half belonged to whoever was in power. His fellow magi nodded their agreement.

The third astrologer peered out from his fantastic turban to say, "We told the king we would return to him when we found the child we sought. But we go instead back to our homes where the people of Israel are spread across lands far from the holy city. To them we will carry the good news. And perhaps the king will wait for our return until some other matters occupy him, and your child, the savior of our people, will be safe."

Then each of the astrologers produced a gift from within his robes. The first, the restless one, handed Mary an ornate, silver box.

When she lifted the lid, the sweet smell of frankincense filled the room, and Mary smiled her thanks. The second and tallest magus produced a corked jar. This myrrh will heal most wounds was all he said. Again Mary smiled, though with less pleasure, Ozeret observed. The third astrologer handed a bag to Joseph. "Take this gold," he said, "and use it to raise the child in all the wisdom that gold may purchase. He must learn the words of the prophets that he find his path and lead us to salvation."

Ozeret watched Mary glaring at the tall magus while he spoke to her husband. Joseph bowed his thanks and then placed the bag of gold beside the other gifts in his wife's lap.

Then the baby woke and started to wail. Ozeret smelled what he had done and was not surprised to see the magi bow their way out of the room as quickly as they could. Mary signaled to Ozeret, and she came and took each gift and secured it in the donkey's panniers hanging by the door. Then she lifted the squalling infant and carried him to the corner where she changed his soiled linens and then returned him to his mother. Ozeret carried the linens to the courtyard to soak in an iron pot and then hurried down the street to catch a final glimpse of the camels as they turned a corner and headed east to their homes far from Herod's reach.

THE NEXT DAY Judas darted from alley to alley with his hood pulled tightly around his head. He knew he must get back to Jerusalem and wanted to speak with Ozeret before he left. He accosted her on her way to the well and pulled her into a doorway out of sight of the street. He questioned her about his son's size and cry and appetite. He asked if his son had the gift he had bought and who had come to the inn with camels and a full retinue of servants.

Finally he stopped talking. He saw that Ozeret was staring at him with both amazement and disgust on her face.

Judas hung his head and felt ashamed. "I ask your forgiveness," he said. "I think only of myself. I forget to thank you for your great service to my son and his mother."

He watched Ozeret's face and was relieved to see her relax. She reached out and touched the obsidian that hung on a leather cord around his neck. It glowed even in the shadowy doorway.

Judas smiled. "This is my talisman," he said. It is my birth sign and is with me in my darkest hours. People fear the scorpion, Ozeret," he went on. "They fear its sting and pretend that they can avoid life's pain."

Judas paused and felt darkness snaking towards him from the depths of the alley. But then Ozeret reached inside her tunic and pulled out the smooth, black obsidian he had given her to keep for his son. She stroked the scorpion etched into its surface and then held an imaginary baby in her arms and rocked the child. Judas stood watching until his mind was clear and calm.

In another week, Joseph led the donkey, with Mary and her son and the bulging panniers, out of Bethlehem and past the stable for the journey home. Ozeret walked behind carrying a bundle on her head and a basket on her arm. She glanced at Judas when he peered out from a bush beside the path after the donkey passed.

Judas restrained himself from speaking to her and had to content himself with following them until the gates of the city appeared. He waited until they had passed through the gates and then made his way, reluctantly, to the dismal house where Seth would, undoubtedly, sting him with rebukes and shame.

CHAPTER 11

Jerusalem

Forty days after the birth of his son, Judas waited near the entrance to the Temple. He watched Mary, radiant in her blue cape and crimson gown and regal as a queen, process up the hill with his son in her arms.

Judas didn't dare enter the Temple. His notoriety as a Zealot fighting the Roman oppressors was growing, and he knew he would have to leave the city soon. In fact Seth had ordered him to leave several days before. But first he had to bear witness to his son's acceptance into the world which had always ostracized his father.

Judas didn't dare mount the Temple steps and watch the presentation of his son to the priests. He had to leave that to Joseph, who walked slowly, shoulders bowed and eyes downcast, behind Mary and her son. Joseph carried the two doves to be offered in a sacrifice of thanksgiving; Judas could not claim that task. But Judas knew that Ozeret, who saw him in the doorway of a shop and nodded her head, carried the scorpion which was his gift and blessing on this and every day.

While Judas was hiding in the shadows of an alley waiting for his son to emerge from the Temple, he heard two women, bowed with age, whispering as they shuffled down the street leaning on each other. Their lamentation stopped his heart, and he felt darkness enter. For the women were keening in their bird-like voices that King Herod planned to murder every Judean boy under the age of two. They were mourning for the grandsons they knew they had already lost.

Judas didn't know how much time passed after darkness overcame him. He found himself sprawled in the filth of the alley. The sun had moved from overhead to beyond the buildings on the other side of the street. Judas was trembling with the need for action.

He stood up and brushed himself off. When he crept from the alley, his clothes carried its stench. He wanted to leave the city, to rush through the gate to the Mount of Olives and roll in the herb-sweetened hills. Instead he made his way to the street Ozeret travelled each afternoon to fetch water for her family.

Judas huddled in the shadows of the buildings by the street waiting for Ozeret's familiar black cape to appear. When he saw her, he reached out and grabbed her arm pulling her into the shadowy alley. He felt the tremor in her body that spoke as loudly as a scream. He caught her jug as it tumbled from her head and set it on the ground. Then he pulled the hood of her cape from her head and whispered urgently in her ear.

Judas watched Ozeret's face carefully to make sure she understood what he was saying. Then he handed her a writing slat and implored her to make sure Joseph received it before he slept that night.

When night came, Judas crept behind the Roman soldier standing at his post by the city gate that led to the long road to Egypt. Judas garroted the soldier and dragged him outside the city walls. Then Judas and the dead soldier hid behind a rock and began their silent vigil.

Time crept slowly for Judas, each interval filled with worry. What if Joseph disregarded his warning? What would happen to his son?

JERUSALEM LAY SLEEPING under a starless sky. The darkness made Ozeret's fingers clumsy as she fastened the donkey's panniers.

Ozeret knew the risk Judas took that afternoon when he warned her of the danger to his son. His great height and alarming blue eyes stood out wherever he went, and his name was now linked with the Zealots. Ozeret had heard a rumor that there was a price on his head. She knew there were plenty of people in the city who would betray one of their own for a few coins or to gain favor with the ruling oppressors. She feared for his safety but was glad to know he was looking out for the baby. Jerusalem was a dangerous place, full of intrigue and superstitions, and King Herod was an unstable man. He feared for his position and murdered anyone who seemed a threat. And now it seemed little boys were caught in the wide web of his paranoia.

Ozeret had felt the fear that clutched the hearts of the mothers and grandmothers as they waited to fill their jars at the well. She had heard the impotence in the voices of fathers and grandfathers who came to Joseph's shop and spoke angrily to him while she swept up the sawdust to spread below the fig tree in the garden. Even the children she passed in the streets seemed anxious and irritable as the rumors of Herod's rage began to shape the future of each family.

"The rumors are true," Judas had whispered as he filled her jug. "The massacre of every boy under the age of two will begin as soon as Herod's soothsayers discover the most propitious day. Jerusalem's grandmothers already mourn."

Ozeret wondered if Judas had heard what happened that morning at the Temple. If Herod learned of it, the massacre would happen soon. For an old man had taken Jesus from Mary's arms, as she stood before the priest, and announced that he could now die in peace for his eyes beheld the messiah.

Only Ozeret and Mary heard what he whispered as he handed the child back to his mother. He warned her, "Great sorrow shall come to you, mother of our savior." Ozeret had studied Mary's face, but her expression remained calm as always.

Mary moved through each day serenely. She nursed the baby and whispered secrets in his swaddled ear. She wove and sewed tiny garments for him to wear when the swaddling clothes grew too confining. And she spread out a scroll on the table each afternoon and studied the black marks for confirmation of the certainty she shared with the magi who had visited her and then betrayed the king.

The astrologers never returned to Jerusalem to tell Herod where he could find the miraculous child. Ozeret wondered how they knew they should keep his whereabouts a mystery. And she wondered if word had travelled across the winter-deadened hills to their caravan that Herod planned to slaughter every boy who could be the child the astrologers sought. Ozeret wondered what the magi and the old man in the Temple saw in this baby who did exactly what any baby who had lived less than two wanings and waxings of the moon would do.

Mary's baby slept and woke, crying to be fed. He soiled and wet his swaddling clothes, causing Ozeret's hands to redden and crack from their endless immersion in the washing pot. And now he was forcing them to undertake another winter journey far from the comfort of Joseph's house and the peaceful garden whose fig tree would soon leaf out and then bear fruit.

The spice cabinet scented the cold night air. Its presence, strapped to the donkey's side, made this escape from the madness about to descend on Jerusalem, if the rumors about Herod were true, bearable to Ozeret. She remembered how her first mistress once protected the little beggar girl from the temptation of the spice cabinet. Now the key to the spice cabinet was resting securely on its strip of leather between her breasts. If she could guard the spice cabinet, she could protect this baby, the grandson of her first mistress, by teaching him how to escape, like Ozeret, from this world of time and troubles.

Then she noticed the weight of stone beneath her tunic and thought of the scorpion. Dread darkened her heart. What a terrible gift she bore for this precious child.

The child's sling was lined with a woolen blanket to protect him from the frosty night air. Joseph helped Mary onto the donkey and Ozeret handed her the boy. Mary settled the baby into the sling and wrapped her blue robe around both of them. Then Joseph led the donkey, its hooves muffled with rags, down the cobbled street and away from his house and workshop and the fig tree patiently waiting for spring.

JUDAS WATCHED THE little donkey carrying Mary and his son. Joseph walked slowly on one side of the donkey, his shoulders slumped with weariness, and Ozeret on the other.

After the little procession had passed, Judas slid out from his hiding place and followed, always staying in the shadows. He watched his son leave the city through the unguarded gate on the road to Egypt and wept his relief and desolation.

Then he made his way to Ein Karem to warn Elizabeth and Zachariah of the danger to their son.

CHAPTER 12

Egypt

Ozeret walked behind the donkey on the outer edge of the caravan headed to Egypt. She was frightened by the camels that towered above the tiny donkey and wished that Joseph had secured a better position for them. But she knew he was afraid to use the gold the Magi had given his wife. At least they were travelling with a throng of other people. The trek through the Sinai desert would be lonely and dangerous for an old man and his family travelling alone.

The nights were long and cold. Joseph, Mary, and the child slept in a makeshift tent while Ozeret shivered outside, pressed against the flank of the donkey and sharing her thin blanket with the skinny beast.

While the donkey slept and wheezed, Ozeret lay watching the stars and feeling the immensity of the world beyond Jerusalem and Bethlehem and the hills that were all she had ever known. She felt a strange peace overcome her. The fantastic shapes of desert sand that gleamed in starlight and the vast spaces, devoid of streets or buildings or market squares, were oblivious to the cruelties and worries and loneliness that had plagued her since her father dragged her to Jerusalem and abandoned her there. Mary's plans and Joseph's sorrows seemed as tiny and insignificant as a grain of sand in this land beyond the scope of human understanding. Even Herod and the Roman soldiers and the wild, mad Judas seemed frozen and distant in the chill of the endless stars.

Each morning as the child's cries pierced the air and the babble of unfamiliar accents and languages replaced the silence of the night, Ozeret rose stiffly and took her place with the other servants to prepare food for the day. Peace fled with the sun. But she knew that night would come again.

THE HOUSE IN the village where Joseph found lodgings for his wife and her child had rough thick walls of clay to keep out the punishing Egyptian sun. It was just one small room with barely enough space to spread out sleeping pallets. Joseph arranged to exchange his donkey for use of this modest shelter. Then he and Ozeret unloaded the exhausted beast, and its new master led it away.

Mary stood in the doorway of her new home, her expression inscrutable, and watched as Joseph and Ozeret spread out the sleeping pallets and put the cooking pots and Joseph's tools in a corner of the small room. Then she settled herself on her pallet and nursed the child.

Soon their life in Egypt developed a rhythm. Ozeret prepared their meals outside, as soon as there was daylight, and spread her pallet to sleep on the flat thatched roof after night fell. Joseph dozed through the heat of the day, only stirring to eat or relieve himself beyond the trees that ringed the village. And then he slept through the night, sunk in a torpor so profound Ozeret feared for his ever making a life for himself and his family in this strange land.

During the heat of the day Mary rested with the baby in her arms, engrossed in her own thoughts. But each night when the worst of the heat had passed and the air began to cool, Mary rose from her pallet and handed the child to Ozeret. Then she walked for an hour or more, always staying within sight and sound of her child. If the night was bright with moon or stars, she would take a leather slat from her tunic and read as she walked. When the night was dark, she walked with her eyes downcast, a mysterious figure in the silent night. And while his mother walked, the child lay quietly in Ozeret's arms, his brown eyes open and rarely blinking, waiting for his mother to return.

One morning as Ozeret was preparing the day's bread, she saw an old woman clutching a small bundle to her breast stumble down the path that passed through the tiny village. Ozeret knew at once who it was. She rose as quickly as her stiff knees and hips would allow and hurried to the woman.

Elizabeth raised her eyes and smiled her relief. Ozeret took the bundle from her, a baby too light for the months he had been outside his mother's womb, and led the woman to the doorway of the sleeping house. Ozeret unrolled her own pallet and settled mother and son in the narrow space next to where Mary lay. Mary's baby stirred and opened his eyes. Then he and his cousin began to wail their hunger for food and life in this brand-new day.

Elizabeth's wrinkled, sun-scorched face contorted in anguish. Over the hungry cries of her baby, she told of Zachariah's collapse and death just two days out of Ein Karem and of her abandoning him to walk, carrying the baby and leading the exhausted donkey, until the donkey fell to its knees and her milk slowed and then stopped altogether. She described the goatherd who appeared like a mirage on the horizon until he drew closer and discovered her lying against the donkey's flanks with the listless baby drawn close to her barren breasts. As if in a dream, her face soaked in tears and her baby now wailing, she described his milking one of his goats and then twisting a cloth into the warm milk and rubbing the cloth across the baby's mouth. To her astonishment, the baby woke from his torpor and started to suck.

Ozeret heard Mary's voice gently interrupt her cousin's story. "Give the child to me," she said.

Elizabeth rose, trembling with the effort, and handed her son to Mary. Mary settled him with her own boy, one at each breast, and the two babies contentedly nursed.

Calmer now, Elizabeth told of Judas's appearance at her home in Ein Karem and of Zachariah's acceptance of his nephew. And how, hard upon this joy, Judas told them of the need to flee, leaving all behind, before their child was destroyed by Herod. So Zachariah led his wife and son, and all the household furnishings that their donkey could carry, along the long, weary path that travelled from Judea to Egypt.

As Ozeret listened to Elizabeth and sorrowed for the fear and age that etched her face, Joseph rose heavily from his pallet and left the room. Elizabeth watched him and then turned to her cousin.

"How goes it for you in this strange land?" she asked.

Mary sat quietly looking down at the two infants. Then she turned to Elizabeth and smiled. "Out of Egypt our savior must come," she said. "I have read it and know that it is true."

Elizabeth looked confused, but she smiled back at Mary. "I rejoice to have my son join yours," she said, "and hope their paths shall always intertwine."

But then she cried out in agony and clutched at her chest. When Ozeret rushed over to help her, she felt the old woman's spirit fly past her face and knew that what now lay on the pallet was just flesh and brittle bones.

They buried Elizabeth in a grove of sycamore trees and planted a sapling to mark her resting place. Joseph carved a branch he cut from a huge, gnarled tree, shaping its knobby top into a beehive in honor of Elizabeth who saved the life of her son.

CHAPTER 13

Egypt, four years later

News of Herod's death made its way from Jerusalem to the small Egyptian village where Joseph and his family still lived in their crowded clay house.

At first Joseph rejoiced. He missed the comforts of his home and workshop and was eager to return to Jerusalem. The past four years had been hard. He had the responsibility of two young boys and a young wife and was barely able to eke out a living by taking occasional jobs at nearby Heliopolis. The people of that city had not welcomed his family on their flight from Herod, and Joseph felt like a servant when he had to travel there seeking work. But work he must.

The Magi's gift of gold hidden at the bottom of Mary's cedar chest was useless in this foreign land. He feared the dangerous attention it would attract if he tried to use it for food and wine and linen for new clothes. But back home in Jerusalem he could exchange the gold at one of the money lenders' shops at the foot of the Temple Mount and have an abundance of denerii for taxes to the Roman overlords and shekels for the Temple priests. He could send Ozeret to the finest market near Herod's palace to buy indigo for dyeing a new mantle for Mary. It pained him to see his wife dressed in a frayed tunic with the color of her mantle fading under this foreign sun.

Joseph had lost patience with living as a supplicant in a foreign land with its obelisks and strange picture writing and gods so different from the god of his own city.

Joseph rarely stopped to consider the loneliness of his marriage. He had always been lonely, except when Mary was a small child who knew no better than to love him because he loved her. And he had always obeyed others, first his father and older brothers and now this reserved young woman.

Still, he was not prepared for Mary's announcement at their midday meal while the boys messily ate the lentils Ozeret wrapped in the middle of their bread. Mary looked up from her bowl and said calmly, "It is good that we can return to our land, Joseph, and raise our son in Nazareth."

Joseph felt himself grow cold, and the sounds of the boys chattering over their meal receded. And then outrage, fierce and passionate and over as quickly as a bolt of summer lightning, made him rise quickly from his chair and rush from the claustrophobic room.

By the time he was standing, shaking and shuddering in the glare of the midday sun, he felt empty again and knew his wife's will would prevail. They would go to Nazareth, just as they went to Bethlehem, because she was privy to the destiny of her son and he was too weak to speak for his own destiny. Because he had none.

Joseph went back into the room. He could hear the shuffle of his sandals as he went to his corner and sat on his pallet. He felt a hand on his shoulder. Ozeret was leaning down, concern deepening the wrinkles around her eyes and mouth. She handed him his bowl. Joseph shook his head and closed his eyes and tried to escape into sleep from what lay ahead.

CHAPTER 14

Nazareth

Mary had relatives in this small village in Galilee, a branch of her mother's family who had never found their way to Jerusalem. They showed Mary and Joseph an abandoned house, its roof gone and its walls in need of chinking. But it had four rooms and a courtyard and a neglected garden with a fig tree that reminded Ozeret of Joseph's home in Jerusalem. She was glad when Joseph decided to repair the house and garden.

After four years in a foreign land, Ozeret was comforted by the sound of Aramaic spoken in the streets and at the spring and in the tiny market, even if was spoken with a different accent than in Jerusalem. She was pleased to have the spice chest hanging once again in the room where she slept and to have a roof over her head instead of sky and changing weather.

At night she lay breathing in the complexity of the spice chest and listening to the whispers and muffled laughter of the two little boys. Their liveliness distracted her from the silence behind the other curtain where Mary and Joseph lay.

She ached in sympathy for Joseph. At first he was busy repairing the house and thatching the roof. All spring, as the hills around the village swayed with dancing wildflowers and the fig tree in the garden leafed out, he seemed content to be useful in repairing the house for his family. During the summer months he used the extra room as his workshop and built beds and chairs and a table to replace what had been left behind four years before. But when summer was over and the rains that spoke of winter began, he grew silent and moody, even with the boys, and spent his days in the gloomy workshop, which had only one small northern window. Ozeret brought his food and wine to him there and worried about his idleness.

Nazareth couldn't support a carpenter with Joseph's skill. No one had the taste or wealth for Joseph's finely crafted tables and chairs. Most people ate their meals sitting on the stones or hard-packed dirt inside their drafty homes. They needed milking stools and doors and timbers for their roofs, not chairs and tables and wooden toys for their children. They lacked the luxury to want more than they had. Joseph bartered his time and the roughest use of his skilled hands and fine tools for wool and food and wine.

Despite her anxiety about Joseph, Ozeret rejoiced in Mary's son Jesus and his cousin John. They were noisy and happy and oblivious to the sad and aging man and his solemn, silent wife. They ran back and forth, falling down and skinning their knees in the streets, when Ozeret went to buy food in the market. They tracked in mud and joy and the world outside the lonely house. During meals they spilled their food and nudged each other while Jesus made up ridiculous stories about what they had seen and heard in the town that day. Even Mary looked up from her food to smile at her son's foolishness though Joseph, on the rare occasions when he joined them at mealtime, just glowered.

Mary's son was long-limbed and more delicate than his cousin and, though taller than John, followed his lead in everything but the telling of stories.

When Jesus described the three-legged cat that lived in the alley by the marketplace, Ozeret recognized its narrow eyes and the dogged grace of its stealth as it darted out to seize a scrap of food that fell from a cart or basket. When he told his mother that he and John had flown to Jerusalem on the wings of an eagle and gathered figs from her mother's tree for her to eat, Ozeret felt the spirit of her first mistress, her childhood savior, in the boy who followed John around the little village. Jesus filled her heart and mind with the stories she had forgotten she missed.

Ozeret cared for John, mending his tunic and cleaning his scrapes, but her heart could not reach him. He was a stocky five-year-old, without the long-limbed grace of Jesus, and could be as commanding and solemn as Zachariah. He seemed guided by voices Ozeret couldn't hear and too serious for a little boy who had a roof over his head and food in his belly, even if he had no parents to call his own. Ozeret wondered if his heart felt orphaned like her own.

As soon as the rains ended and the garden mud returned to dirt, Mary took the boys out each morning and taught them the letters that formed the words that were more real to her than flesh and tears. While the streets outside the garden rang with the shouts and laughter of Nazareth's children, Mary schooled the cousins, not releasing them until they had satisfied her with their progress in scratching symbols in the dirt. Then they ran and hopped and skipped their way to the market with Ozeret, sometimes pausing to grumble about their wasted morning in the garden while the other boys, too young for the synagogue, were free to play.

CHAPTER 15

Jerusalem

That spring Joseph fastened the panniers to the donkey in preparation for the trip to Jerusalem. Mary was adamant that he take her son to the Temple for Passover and see if, by some miracle, the scrolls they had abandoned when they fled to Egypt five years before were still safely hidden. She admonished him to take some of the gold the astrologers had given them in Bethlehem and exchange it for coins at the Temple. They were growing poor in Nazareth, and the gold was useless to them there. No one had coins to exchange for gold, and the knowledge that they possessed such wealth would put them in danger of robbery or worse.

He wondered why Mary was unwilling to make the journey, but she insisted that she and John and the servant would stay in Nazareth. Perhaps Mary's god had dictated this plan, Joseph thought bitterly. But he was too tired to hold onto his anger for long.

Joseph often forgot that Jesus was trudging along beside him. He was wrapped up in his own thoughts and aches and pains, and the boy never uttered a word. But when they stopped at midday, with the crowd of the villagers heading to Jerusalem for the week of Passover, the boy settled himself on the same rock, and Joseph remembered to hand him bread and give him a long sip from the water flask.

When night fell, Joseph took his bedroll from the donkey's side and unrolled it under the overhang of a rock. The boy settled next to him and suddenly, under the starlit sky with the air scented by spring flowers and herbs, Joseph felt his body relax and his mind quicken. The darkness that had enveloped his spirit for so many years lifted a bit and he put his arm around the boy to shield him from the cool night air.

Joseph wondered if Jesus was lonely, separated from his cousin and his mother and the servant who had cared for him since the day he was born. Feeling the child's misery and, brushing his cheek, feeling tears, Joseph hugged him closer.

Suddenly the boy unleashed a torrent of questions. They all began with "why."

"Why does my mother know how to read and teach me and my cousin while all around us the women and children work and play without studying words?"

"Why are you so old?"

"Why does Ozeret not speak?"

And then, reaching into his tunic, he pulled out a polished stone that glistened in the starlight. "Why must I wear a scorpion, most deadly of stinging creatures, around my neck both day and night? It frightens me, but Ozeret gave it to Mother this morning, and Mother says I must wear it all my life."

Joseph wanted to fashion answers that would satisfy the little boy whose mind and speech were as agile as his limbs. But finally all he could say was, "Perhaps you should speak with your mother when we return from Jerusalem, or, when you are older, you will discover the answers for yourself."

Joseph could feel his own final darkness fast approaching as he lay in the cold of early morning watching the stars disappear and the sky turn gray. He worried for this child and for the child's cousin John and for his wife who was now on a mission that swept up everyone in her path. He could not guess what the future would bring, and he knew he would be gone before it unfolded.

When they arrived in Jerusalem, Joseph led the boy and donkey through the streets to his abandoned home. The door was still locked, and, when he opened it, all was dank and dusty but exactly as he had left it years before. So they left their belongings and went to the Temple to exchange their gold.

The streets were crowded with visitors come to Jerusalem to celebrate the Passover. Merchants lined the Temple courtyards selling wares from every place that the exiled people of Israel had fled over centuries of oppression and strife. Joseph's heart lifted. He had almost forgotten the city of his birth. Perhaps he would sharpen his carving tools when he returned to Nazareth. Here was a market for his finest pieces.

The money changers were doing a brisk trade in coins from every corner of the world. Joseph circled their stalls twice, not sure who would give him the best exchange for his nuggets of gold. As he stood looking around, a tall man with his face hidden within his brown cloak approached.

"Are you Joseph, now of Nazareth?" the man asked. Joseph was startled by the blue of the man's eyes as he bent down to speak.

"Yes," Joseph answered. He paused as a memory came to him. A tall young man in a shepherd's tunic broke his staff across his knee and then ran wildly from the gathering of the suitors on the day of Mary's betrothal. "And who are you?"

"Please speak with me," the man begged. "I am Judas, the man raised by your wife's cousin Elizabeth, and I would be glad to hear how your family fares."

Joseph held Jesus's hand more firmly. He wondered how much Judas knew. Did he know that Elizabeth and Zachariah both died on the journey to Egypt? Did he know that Elizabeth's son John was in Nazareth? And how, Joseph wondered, did he recognize them? Joseph knew his own appearance had changed since the betrothal. He was now a stooped old man. And Jesus had not yet been born when he last saw Judas.

"My home is very simple and crowded," Judas said. "May we speak where you are staying?"

Joseph's uneasiness grew. Should he lead this man to his home? But how could he turn away a man who had been raised by Mary's cousin. So Joseph nodded and led Judas back through the streets near the Temple, with their enormous houses and fine markets, until they came to his own modest neighborhood of artisans and shopkeepers.

They sat in the garden for the day was warm and fair. Joseph apologized for offering no refreshment, explaining that they had not yet been to the market to buy food. A look of concern passed over Judas's face. "Has the boy not eaten?" he asked.

Joseph realized it had been several hours since their simple meal of figs and goat cheese at dawn before they came to the city. He looked at the boy who was idly digging in the ground under the fig tree. "Are you hungry?" he called to the child.

Jesus looked up and nodded.

Joseph's heart sank. How could he have forgotten the needs of the child? "I must change money for the market," he explained miserably. "That's why we were at the Temple."

Judas got up and pulled a purse from his tunic. "Take this," he ordered "and fetch food for us. I'll stay with the child. It saddens me to know so little of him and of his mother and of the child born to her cousin who raised me."

Joseph felt himself torn in two directions. He didn't want to leave the boy with a stranger, but the stranger was the foster child of Mary's cousin. He couldn't ask a visitor to go buy refreshments for his home. Borrowing the money was shameful enough. And so, feeling he had no choice, Joseph nodded his agreement and set off for the simple market that sold bread and fruit and cheese.

When Joseph returned, the boy was chattering to the stranger as if he had always known him. The stranger, Judas, was smiling at the child, his blue eyes so bright Joseph wondered if they were holding back tears. With a troubled mind, Joseph set out the simple meal, and the three of them ate and drank on the bench under the fig tree.

When the meal was over, Judas said he must go. Joseph begged him to go back to the Temple with them and help him choose a money lender. He insisted that he must repay Judas. A look of unspeakable sadness passed over Judas's face as he refused. "You have repaid me by this visit," he said simply. "But I can tell you the man who will give you full value for your gold."

Joseph stiffened. How did Judas know he had gold to exchange and not some other coins?

Judas went on, "I keep the purse for my fellow Zealots as we fight to free our people from the Roman yoke. So I know the money lenders and can advise you who will treat you with honesty and respect."

Joseph's head was swimming. This man was a Zealot, enemy of Herod and the priests who curried the favor of Rome? Would he and Mary's child get caught up in his treasonous acts?

As if he could read Joseph's mind, Judas spoke reassuringly. "No one knows I am here. No one will know we have spoken. I will describe the man you should seek out at the Temple and then I shall disappear."

After Judas left, Joseph watched the boy stroke the obsidian stone around his neck. Joseph felt tired and confused. But he took the boy's hand and led him back to the Temple where he exchanged gold nuggets for enough coins for food and a sacrificial lamb for Passover and the needs of his household in Nazareth.

THE BOY WAS filled with excitement from the moment his eyes flew open in the morning until he fell into an exhausted, dreamless sleep at night. The city was enormous, as if fifty of his villages were joined together in a maze of streets and sounds and smells. He heard people speak Aramaic with an accent so different from the people in his village. Here everyone sounded like his mother and Joseph. And he heard people speak languages he didn't know. Joseph explained that there were visitors from every direction come to gather at the greatest building in the world to remember their history and celebrate their god's care for them. Some of these people lived far away in lands with different sights and sounds and ways of speaking. But they all worshipped the god of this temple.

After they broke their fast, Joseph and Jesus went to the little shed attached to Joseph's house to fetch the lamb they had purchased in the market the day before. They fed it and filled a bucket with fresh water. Then Joseph fastened both doors to the shed, top and bottom. Jesus could hear the lamb bleating. "He wants to see the sky," the boy said.

Joseph shook his head. "We need him for the Passover feast, and I don't want someone to steal him for their own sacrifice. He must stay locked away."

The sound of the lamb's cries followed them down the street and drained the day of its joy. But when they turned a corner and joined a throng of chattering pilgrims speaking a foreign tongue and smelling of unfamiliar food, Jesus's spirits rose again. He took Joseph's hand and smiled up at the old man.

Soon they came to a house where Joseph pulled the boy into the doorway and knocked on the wooden door. A woman opened the door and, heeding Joseph's request, led them through the courtyard into the room where the family was still breaking its fast. Jesus looked around and saw a man even older than Joseph but with the same nose and brow. The man stood up when he saw them enter and said, in a voice without any warmth, "So you have returned to us at last and brought your wife's son with you. Do you stay or is your home now Nazareth?"

The two young men sitting at the table laughed at this, and the children looked up from their food to find out what could be the joke. Jesus moved behind Joseph. He felt shamed and scared in this room and wondered why they had come.

"Brother," he heard Joseph say. "I come to pay my respects to you as the eldest son in our family. Mary's son and I have come for Passover and to take what we need from the house where we once lived. Then it is yours to use as you see fit."

Jesus was shocked to hear Joseph's brother laugh scornfully. "As you can see, Joseph," he said, as his arm swept around the spacious room with its painted walls and carpets on the floor, "I have no need for the house where we were raised. My family and the families of my sons live well in the house my trade has built. But I shall tell our brothers of your offer. They are not as successful as I and still ply our father's craft throughout the city."

And then, without offering Joseph either food or drink, he returned to his meal.

As he followed Joseph out of the room, Jesus was puzzled and troubled. In the street he took Joseph's hand and walked with him back to the house. He watched the old man sit silently at the table through the rest of the morning and into the afternoon. Finally, when his stomach's rumbling would give him no peace, Jesus tugged on Joseph's sleeve and asked for food.

After they ate a bit of bread, they went to the shed and fastened a rope around the lamb's neck. Then Jesus followed Joseph and the lamb back to the Temple.

Despite the gloom of Joseph and the bleating of the lamb, Jesus felt his spirits rise again. This was very different from the Passover celebration in Nazareth. The Temple courtyard was so huge, and the marble altar, already bloody, gleamed in the afternoon sun. He and Joseph and the lamb waited their turn. Then Joseph slit the lamb's throat, and a priest caught its blood in a bowl and flung the blood against the altar. Joseph stripped the lamb of its skin and carried a portion of its fat, along with its organs, to another priest who burned them on the altar. Then he and Jesus left the Temple to roast the flesh of the lamb at home.

The smell of roasting flesh and bitter herbs made Jesus feel his hunger. He had a memory of the year before with his mother and his cousin and his mother's people all celebrating together. He wished that he had family in this grand city, family that would welcome him and include him in the feast.

Joseph prepared the Passover meal with unleavened bread and bitter herbs and a bowl of nuts and fruits mixed with honey. After the second cup of wine, Joseph told Jesus to ask, "Why is this night different from all others?" He listened as Joseph told of a people in bondage in Egypt and how their god rescued them and brought them to a land of milk and honey. His head was beginning to feel fuzzy from the wine, even though Joseph watered his goblet generously. He missed his mother and his cousin and Ozeret.

Before they had filled their cups a third time, there was a knock on the door. Joseph shuffled over to open it. Outside stood Judas.

Jesus was glad to have another person at their lonely feast and pulled an extra chair to the table. Joseph took a goblet from the shelf that held extra plates and bowls and wiped away the dust on his tunic. Then he filled it and handed it to Judas.

The men and boy moved through the rest of the Seder. Jesus was relieved when they got to the last psalm and the last lines. With Joseph and Judas he gave thanks for goodness and mercy.

In silence Joseph and Judas and Jesus drank one more cup of wine. Then Joseph spoke the final blessing and pulled his purse out of his tunic. He counted out the money Judas had lent him the day before. Jesus watched Judas hesitate before he took the coins from Joseph's outstretched hand and put them in his own purse.

Jesus felt sleepy from the wine and the heavy meal and the homesickness that filled his eyes with tears. He felt his head grow heavy. Strong arms lifted him and gently placed him on his pallet. He felt the warmth of the blanket cover him and then nothing more.

CHAPTER 16

Nazareth

While Joseph unloaded and fed the tired donkey, Jesus rushed into the house to find his mother. She was sitting at the table as he burst through the door. "We got your scrolls, Mother, and lots of shekels and shared the Passover feast with a man called Judas. He helped us get the shekels and, Mother, he has a scorpion just like mine." Jesus pulled the stone from under his tunic and smiled happily at his mother.

Mary sat quietly. Jesus felt her gaze on him and squirmed anxiously. Why wasn't she smiling at him as she usually did?

Jesus turned from his mother and ran to Ozeret. He flung his arms around her. His head was already higher than her waist. He felt her hand smooth his hair and looked up for her smile.

Then he looked around the room and asked, "Where's John?" He was tired of spending all his time with adults and wanted to play in the courtyard with his cousin.

Mary called him to her side. "Your cousin has gone to live with some relatives far from here," she said. "They came for him while you were gone."

Jesus looked at her in disbelief and then rushed into the room he shared with John. His cousin's pallet and chest of clothes were gone.

Jesus ran to the shelf that Joseph had built to hold the family's dishes and cups. John's bowl and cup were gone.

Jesus collapsed into a heap in front of the table. He felt Ozeret's arms around him but struggled to get free. Then he ran out of the house and down the dusty street until a stitch in his side stopped him.

Jesus felt a hand on his arm. He looked up and saw a relative of his mother, a man who sometimes came to the house to share the olives he harvested from his trees on the hillside above the village. The man addressed him in the dialect that sounded so different from the speech in Jesus's home and the speech he heard in Jerusalem. But the man's voice was kind.

Jesus wiped his face with the back of his hand. "My cousin is gone," was all he could manage to say.

The man nodded. "I saw him leave," he told the boy. "He is to live by the Salt Sea where men hate the Temple priests. Your mother sent him there. I am sorry to think of you without your cousin. You and your mother are strange to us, and you will be a lonely child. But your mother does what she wills."

Then the man took Jesus's hand and led him back to the house where his mother greeted them with her serene smile. "You will meet your cousin again," she promised Jesus, "when you are both men. But your childhood and his have parted. Accept this sorrow and school yourself to be strong and brave."

The man ruffled Jesus's hair and then left without a word to Mary. "Go play in the garden," Mary said "until it is time to go to market with Ozeret. Tomorrow your lessons with me will begin again."

CHAPTER 17

Jerusalem, five years later

Jerusalem felt cramped and claustrophobic, and the noise hurt Ozeret's ears. She had not been back since the night, so long ago, when they fled from Herod's insane massacre. Now the baby they had carried to Egypt was as tall as his mother, all long arms and legs and enormous eyes that never seemed to blink.

They stayed with one of Joseph's brothers, an ancient man who had moved into Joseph's house with his widowed daughter when his wife died and his mind started to fade. Ozeret heard the daughter tell Mary in a choked voice how her father had been scorned by his older brother and shamed into seeking refuge away from the house the rest of the family shared. Ozeret ached for the man and for his daughter. Though they had a roof over their heads, they seemed as lonely and outcast as she had been before her first mistress gave her a place in her home. She was glad to see that Jesus spoke with respect to the old man, even when spittle flew from his lips and he reeked of the accidents that soiled his linens. She was proud of the boy when he asked his father to give the widow a nugget of the gold they had brought to change into shekels.

Joseph sold his carved bowls and plates to the visitors who swarmed through the Temple courtyards. Ozeret was glad when he returned home in the evening with a straighter back and firmer walk. He had worked all year on the wares he could sell in Jerusalem and seemed proud to have his craftsmanship honored in this place.

One day Mary took Jesus to visit her mother's relatives, a cousin and her family who lived in a handsome house near Herod's palace. Ozeret was astonished by the opulence of painted walls and lavish lamps and the delicate food and drink placed before them on silver plates and platters. She felt plain and drab as she stood with the servants. Their tunics were fine linen. Hers was coarse cotton.

They whispered in the refined Aramaic of Judea. Ozeret realized her thoughts had taken on the cruder accents of Galilee.

The visit was brief and unsatisfactory. Mary's cousin questioned her about Nazareth and asked Jesus about his town. Ozeret saw that the woman was trying to humiliate them. Though Jesus now studied with the rabbi at Nazareth's synagogue, Mary's cousin made sure to point out the superior qualification of her sons' teachers in their neighborhood synagogue and the lavishness of festivals at the Temple. She asked Mary about her home and servants. Mary answered simply and honestly and seemed indifferent to the looks her cousin exchanged with her daughters who appeared to be unfamiliar with the workings of loom and spinning wheel and to despise a relative who performed these homely tasks herself.

For the rest of the week of Passover, Ozeret and the boy explored the city while Mary stayed at home with the old man and his daughter. Ozeret enjoyed these outings with the boy. His presence dispelled the discomfort she felt among such crowds with their unfamiliar sounds and smells. Although he was too old now to hold her hand, he was careful never to stray from her side. He seemed both exhilarated and overwhelmed by the crowds drawn to Jerusalem to celebrate the Passover and escape the monotony of their small villages and familiar neighbors. He stopped to touch fine fabrics and silver jewelry in the elegant market near King Herod's palace and stooped to sniff unfamiliar spices and taste plump dates in the more utilitarian stalls in the older part of the city. The whole of Jerusalem, its grand buildings and its hovels, its priests and its soldiers, its elegant ladies and street urchins all had equal claim on his curiosity.

Whenever they passed a beggar or a cripple or a mother whose child had eyes glazed with hunger, Jesus implored Ozeret to give them a coin or some of the food they had purchased. When she rebuked him with a look, he just smiled and assured her there would be enough. "For you, Ozeret, can work your magic on what we bring home," he would say. "There will be enough for all if you so will it." Ozeret loved the sound of her name on the boy's tongue and, while scowling at him, did what he asked.

Each afternoon, after Ozeret scraped the plates into her own cracked bowl and scoured the table and the family's plates and goblets, she ate her own portion of food and then wrapped bread and cheese and fruit in a linen cloth and walked up the hill with the boy to bring food to Joseph in the market.

She rejoiced to see him away from the burdens of his home.

He looked much younger a man than he did within the confines of the house in Nazareth. His face lit up when he saw them, and he asked Jesus what he had learned about the city that day. Jesus sat with him as he ate his meal and told him about the buildings and people of the city. Often Joseph could add to the boy's growing store of knowledge. He knew the city well. He had run errands for his father in every quarter and had worked on some of Herod's building projects. Ozeret was happy to watch Jesus look at this man, so quiet and humble in his own home, as a wise and important part of this world apart from his mother's domain.

Sometimes Jesus would wander away from the courtyard to other parts of the Temple where only Jewish men and boys were allowed. Then Joseph would eat his meal in silence, hand Ozeret the empty basket, and motion her away. Desolation overtook Ozeret. She remembered that she didn't belong anywhere. She was not one of this god's people, and the family she served was not her own.

Ozeret walked behind Joseph's donkey on the path that led from Jerusalem back to Nazareth. The donkey's burden was much lightened by Joseph's success in the Temple market. Mary was some distance away, walking among a group of women from Nazareth, silent as usual amidst their excited chatter about Jerusalem and the Passover festival. They were all part of a multitude of people travelling home to the villages and tiny settlements of Judea and Galilee. Ozeret trudged along with the sounds of different accents and dialects swirling around her. She lagged further and further behind Joseph and suddenly realized that she had fallen to the back of the crowd. Exhaustion overcame her. She missed the lively company of Jesus and wondered where he was.

Then someone spoke her name. "Ozeret, my son is in the Temple still. Give this to his mother."

Ozeret turned and saw the tall figure of Judas, his head uncovered and gleaming in the sun. His blue eyes held hers for a moment and then he pressed a piece of parchment into her hand and disappeared into the hills.

Ozeret looked down at the black marks on the parchment. At the bottom she made out a drawing of a scorpion. Fear for the boy seized her, and she ran along the edge of the crowd. She couldn't see Mary and the women from Nazareth, but she finally caught a glimpse of Joseph leading his donkey. Ozeret forced her way through the crowd until she was beside him. Panting with exhaustion and fear, she pressed the note into his hand.

Joseph lifted his tired, lined face and looked at her in surprise. Then he looked down at the parchment. His face turned ashen. He thrust the reins into Ozeret's hands and went in search of Mary.

When Judas got back to the Temple, shadows were lengthening in the courtyard where his son still sat, surrounded by Temple priests. Judas stood behind a column with his hood drawn over his face and listened.

Judas was awed by the authority in his son's voice. Jesus was only twelve years old and yet the priests listened to him as if he were a prophet from the scrolls of their holy scriptures. Jesus spoke of a day soon to come when the god of the Temple would reveal his true nature to his people and they would be saved from the sorrow and death of this world. The priests listened raptly as the boy, his voice still as high and lilting as a child's, used the words from their holy scrolls to explain how they had fashioned a god of their own making, a god of floods and rainbows and laws carved in stone. He told them the god of their Temple would always be beyond their reach and unable to help them. The true god was within each of them. When the messiah they awaited came among them, he would show them the way to this truth, and they would be saved.

A group of Roman soldiers appeared at the far end of the corridor that led to the courtyard, ignoring the sign that forbade Gentiles from proceeding. Judas slipped away.

CHAPTER 18

Nazareth

Worry tightened Ozeret's chest as she plodded towards Nazareth leading the donkey. Why did the boy stay behind in Jerusalem? When would Mary and Joseph return home?

Despair overcame her. The little girl she once was, abandoned and alone, woke up and looked and listened and was afraid. That child had never fully trusted the home she was led to many years before or the home of Mary and Joseph. She had always believed her true station in this world was to be huddled against a wall or cringing in an alley, alone and unprotected.

Ozeret lay well apart from the crowd that night, keeping guard over the donkey and the family's possessions. She was too worried to eat and only took a few sips from the goatskin carrying water for the journey.

They arrived at Nazareth late the next day. Ozeret unloaded the donkey and led her to the stable. She lowered the donkey's bucket into the cistern in the courtyard and drew back from the frightened face she saw reflected there. Anxiety shortened her breath. Where were her people? She unpacked the panniers and hung them in Joseph's workshop. She spread the blankets on the garden wall to air.

Late that night, as she lay huddled in wakeful misery, the door opened and the smells of a night journey mingled with the familiar scent of the room. Ozeret sprung up and lit the oil lamp in the middle of the table.

The boy looked chastened and tired. He headed straight to his bed chamber. Joseph hung up his cloak and followed him.

Ozeret studied her mistress as she sat immobile in her dusty travelling cloak staring at her own private world. In the lamp light her face looked pinched. Fine lines of worry radiated from the corners of her eyes. Ozeret realized that Mary's son had taken the first step on a perilous journey.

Joseph came back into the main room and stood for a moment with his hand resting gently on Mary's head. Ozeret's eyes met Joseph's, and she saw a grief and dread too deep for words. Then Joseph extinguished the lamp and went to his bed chamber, leaving Mary to keep vigil over the future she had set in motion for her son and could no longer control.

Each day Ozeret watched Joseph as he slowly ate his meals and cared for the donkey. Her bones ached in sympathy when he was summoned to repair rotten timbers or frame new doorways. They were both growing old, and their bodies were ill suited to hard work and undue exertion.

Spring turned to summer. The brilliant anemones that blanketed the hills of Galilee gave way to heat and drought. The villagers moved slowly and listlessly through the rounds of drawing the last of the water from the cisterns in their courtyards, tending their sheep and gardens, and preparing simple meals. Jerusalem with its bustling streets and vast Temple seemed lifetimes away.

Sometimes Ozeret would open the spice cabinet just to smell the exotic seasonings Joseph had allowed her to buy at the spice market in the Temple. She knew she was squandering their essential oils and heard the reproving voice of her first mistress. But now, as she was growing old, she felt an authority within her that gave her permission to enjoy this pleasure from time to time.

The boy asked about the herbs and spices she used. He seemed as indifferent as his mother to the food itself but enjoyed its preparation. He often begged to open the spice cabinet and take out the tiny jars so he could sniff their contents. She indulged him, suspecting that his grandmother would have allowed her grandson this extravagance.

Ozeret taught Jesus to arrange the seeds in the cabinet by size and shape—cardamom, dill, fennel and the rest—always ending with the tiny mustard seed. In this way he would learn the power locked within the smallest of creation. Perhaps someday he would grow beyond Nazareth and achieve greatness. His mother thought he would.

As Ozeret grew old and slept less and less at night, she thought about this family. Joseph loved the feel and look of the wood he crafted. Mary lived among the words on her scrolls. And the boy delighted in every smell and sight and sound in his world. They were very different from the villagers who seemed to move through their days as indifferently and stoically as Joseph's donkey.

Ozeret's watched Joseph grow more stooped each day. His hands, like her own, were stiffening with age. He could no longer carve the tiny sheep and goats and donkeys that had delighted Mary's childhood and fetched a good price in Jerusalem.

Jesus had no talent with wood or interest in making it useful or beautiful. Ozeret knew this was another sorrow Joseph had to bear. Joseph taught Jesus to smooth and oil and polish what he himself made and to assist him in repairing timbers and building doors and windows throughout the town. But the boy remained a dreamy carpenter's apprentice, preferring to study his mother's scrolls or wander through the hills in solitude.

Gradually, Joseph spent more and more time dozing among the dust motes in his shop, refusing new jobs and rarely working on the projects all around him. Ozeret felt him drifting away from them until one day, when Ozeret went to fetch him for the midday meal, all that remained of him was his lifeless body.

Where had he gone, Ozeret wondered, as she helped Mary bathe and anoint him in preparation for his burial. Ozeret followed Jesus and Mary and Mary's cousins as they carried Joseph to the cave in a hill above Nazareth that served as the family burial place. She wondered at Mary's seeming indifference to the loss of her husband and was equally surprised by the vehemence of Jesus's grief.

Jesus sobbed as he carried his corner of the wooden litter that bore Joseph's frail body wrapped in its linen shroud. His cousins glanced at him from time to time as if surprised at this emotion from a boy old enough to have the first hint of a beard darkening his chin. Ozeret wondered if they were capable of any feeling but anticipation of the meal that would follow Joseph's entombment.

Jesus carried Joseph into the crypt and stayed inside its gloom until the family waiting outside grew restless and Mary called, gently but firmly, "It is time for the living to go on, Son."

Jesus appeared, his face pale and his eyes sad. He nodded to his mother and then, with the help of his cousins, rolled the rock over the entrance to the cave.

JESUS LEFT THE next day.

Ozeret woke to his whispered good bye before first dawn. He was kneeling beside her in his travelling cape. He smelled faintly of the little boy he had once been and more powerfully of the man he was becoming. She stared at him through the gloom of the dark room.

"I'm leaving," he said quietly. "Shalom, dear Ozeret." And then he was gone.

Ozeret lay on her pallet as the room brightened. Her mind tried to understand that Joseph and Jesus were both gone. Finally she got up and relieved herself and prepared a meal for Mary. She saw the scrap of parchment the boy left for his mother lying on the table. On the bottom he had drawn the crude outline of a scorpion.

When Mary saw the note, her face was inscrutable. She glanced briefly at Ozeret and then sat down to break her fast. "He will be back," she whispered to herself. "He will be back and he will bring salvation according to our god's plan."

Ozeret moved automatically through her days. She wove the thread Mary spun and cooked and cleaned and fetched water. She bought what they needed from the market. And she worried about Jesus. Who was preparing his meals? Who was bathing his feet? Who was seeing more than a village boy from Nazareth when they looked at the long-limbed, dreamy young man?

There was an abundance of coins from the sale of Joseph's wares at the temple and a generous store of gold from the Magi's gifts still hidden in the bottom of Mary's trunk. And most of their needs could be met by the bartering of Mary's finely woven cloth for olive oil and wine and an occasional portion of meat. Mary was not a destitute widow.

But Ozeret felt bereft without Jesus. Mary never spoke to her or treated her any differently from the donkey growing old in the shed beside the house.

CHAPTER 19

Salt Sea

Jesus had heard stories about the Salt Sea. No fish or plant or frog could live in its waters; for that reason, some called it the Dead Sea. And yet it could bear the weight of a man and carry him on its surface without his doing anything at all.

Jesus needed to be somewhere ruled by death and yet buoyant enough to carry him through the grief he felt at losing Joseph.

When he looked at the worn-out body of Joseph in its linen shroud, he felt himself in the presence of a goodness that could never die. But Joseph was dead. His body was cold, and no breath moved through him. Where could his goodness be? Jesus went to find it.

So he headed towards Jerusalem on the familiar path he followed each Passover, with his mother and Joseph and Ozeret and the people from his village. But before he got to the city, he headed east on a smaller path.

His plan was to follow the Jordan River from the Sea of Galilee all the way to the Sea of Salt. He had heard that holy men went there to find the god who was beyond the control of the Temple priests and the decay of the physical body. He had heard that his cousin John was now one of those holy men.

He headed east to the Sea of Galilee where Joseph took him once to watch the fishermen and learn to catch his supper. They cooked their fish on a fire by the shore and slept to the sound of gentle waves. In the morning two fishermen took Jesus out with them and laughed as he tried to cast their heavy net. He fell overboard and felt the water fill his lungs. Then an arm reached down and pulled him back to the safety of the boat.

When they returned to shore, Joseph was pale with fear and anger. But one of the fishermen put an arm around him and said, "The water will not take this boy of yours. He may sink, but he will always rise again." Then he and the other fisherman walked away, laughing, while Joseph wrapped Jesus in a blanket and set him by the fire until his shivering stopped and he was ready to brag about his adventure.

As Jesus walked along the shore, he wept for Joseph and for himself. Joseph had played the part of his father and yet had not been honored, in life, by the boy he treated as a son.

As the sea narrowed and became the Jordan River, Jesus walked until it was too dark to keep from stumbling over rocks and roots. He slept without remembering his dreams and at sunrise bathed in the river and continued to follow its shore.

As the sun was setting on the second day, the river widened into another sea, and he found himself surrounded by grotesque formations of salt that covered the shoreline like crystal rocks. The salt glinted red and orange until, all at once, the sun disappeared behind a towering wall of rock and Jesus stood peering into the darkening mouths of caves that pierced the cliff above him.

JUDAS DRAGGED THE soldier's body into the bushes to become food for the jackals who roamed the hills by the Salt Sea. The sky was blue and the weather clear, but his mind sizzled. His need to terrorize the Roman oppressors had grown beyond the bounds of the Zealots. He could no longer follow any plan but the twisting path his own compulsions dictated. His body was tired and damaged from so many wounds and so much privation. He had to honor its schedule of energy and profound lethargy. And so he lived and foraged by himself in the caves along the sea.

When the rage overtook his mind and his body was strong enough to follow, he murdered a Roman sentry or a messenger on his way to Masada, the Roman fortress farther south. But most of the time he dozed in the dark recess of a cave, coming out at night to kill some nocturnal animal and fill his goatskin from a freshwater spring above the lake.

At night he dreamed. It was always the same dream, suffusing his senses with warmth and peace and the fragrance of spring grasses. In his dream his son walked towards him. And then they walked together through Zachariah's pasture and sat beside the stream.

Each morning Judas woke slowly to the cold damp of the cave and his loneliness and the aches of his aging body. By the time he was fully awake, the dream had disappeared.

One morning Judas woke and tried to hold onto the dream. He was surprised when the dream stayed with him, so surprised that he stood up and stretched and ventured out of the cave into the bright sunlight of the clear air around the lake.

He had no purpose in leaving the cave. No cloud of rage impelled him to strike a blow against the Roman oppressors or a messenger from the Temple priests. But his very lack of purpose felt compelling and peaceful. He went because he went and walked beside the lake until the stench of his unwashed body caused him to strip and enter the water and scoop up mud to rub himself clean. Then he floated on the surface of the lake while birds swooped and birdsong filled his ears and his body relaxed into trust of the lake's buoyancy.

He must have dozed. When he opened his eyes, his son was standing on the shore staring at him. Judas closed his eyes, willing himself to dream again. But he stayed awake, and when he opened his eyes again, there was Jesus.

Judas swam towards shore and stood. Then, ashamed of his nakedness before his son, he submerged himself to his chin. He heard laughter and saw that Jesus was holding his tunic and beckoning him to the shore.

After Judas covered himself, he stood facing Jesus. The two men looked at each other for a long minute. "Who are you?" Jesus whispered. "Why do you appear when I am most in need?"

Judas shook his head. "I do not know," he answered. "My mother was defiled as a child and died giving birth to me without ever naming the man who so injured her. But I bear his evil."

Judas pulled the obsidian scorpion from inside his tunic and held it in front of Jesus's face. Jesus saw that his hand was shaking.

"I too wear the scorpion." Jesus said. "It stung me when I buried the man who raised me. I did not see his goodness until he was gone. All I saw was that he was not my father."

Jesus stood staring at the shore where salt crystals glittered coldly.

Finally he continued, as if talking to himself. "I seek a guide to teach me to see goodness in others and to save me from the fear of death. When I was a child I went to the Temple and spoke to the priests. Wisdom flowed from me then, like a stream that can withstand the fiercest heat of summer. But now I am a man and feel parched and thirsty."

Jesus paused again and looked at Judas.

"My mother lives," he said. "In that I am more fortunate than you. But she will not tell me who my father is and tries to fashion me into the man she needs her son to be."

Jesus was silent for a long time. Judas stood beside him in the sunlight, aware only of his own joy.

Finally the young man shrugged and put the scorpion back inside his tunic.

"I am glad to have found you, Judas," he said. "When I was hungry in Jerusalem and Joseph forgot to feed me, you made sure I ate. When I missed my mother during the Passover feast, you appeared and your presence comforted me. And now, whenever I feel the smooth stone around my neck, I will remember finding you in this place where men seek god outside the Temple."

Judas looked at his son and wondered what Jesus would think if he knew the truth about his father, that he no longer believed that the god of Israel, or any other god, cared what happened to the people of this world. When Judas looked inside his own heart, he saw the dark cloud of anger and hatred. When he looked at other men, that anger turned to rage. Only when he dreamed of his son, did he feel peace.

And now his son was standing beside him. He should make him leave before he knew the truth and learned to despise him. Then Judas would have no respite from the demons and the scorpion's sting. But his son was here, not just the dream of him. Judas heard his own voice saying, "You may stay with me, though there is danger in that for I am the target of Roman soldiers and Herod's spies."

Jesus laughed a laugh so boyish it made Judas smile. "My life in Nazareth is so devoid of danger or interest of any kind that I welcome a chance to stay here. I tire of rules and rituals and my mother's anxious care."

One day Judas led Jesus to an isolated spot on the shore of the lake where a man sat by himself, stinking of the rank camel skin that was his only clothing. The man's hair was matted and filthy, and his face was so thin that the cheek bones jutted out and the eyes looked sunken and hollow. Jesus didn't recognize his cousin and yet he knew that it was John. Judas had described the man John had become and told Jesus how the fourteen years since he left Nazareth had changed him.

Jesus sat as quietly as his cousin while the air settled around them and the insects resumed their forays. He remembered his childhood in Egypt and Nazareth. He and John were inseparable. Jesus followed John everywhere and imitated his walk and intonation and games. John had been so serious. Jesus couldn't imitate that. But he remembered trying.

As he sat by the Salt Sea under the warm sun, Jesus remembered the desolation he felt when he returned from Jerusalem with Joseph and learned that John was gone. His childhood ended on that day. He felt his mother bearing down, always, molding him into the man she expected him to become. Was John a distraction from his mother's plan? Is that why she had sent him away?

Finally John rose. Jesus stood up and went to him. John stared at him from hollow, red-rimmed eyes and then he embraced Jesus. "You have come," he said. Then he reached out and lifted the leather strap around Jesus's neck. "What is this?" he asked.

Jesus pulled the strap over his head and handed it to John. He watched John as he studied the shiny black stone with its finely etched scorpion. The stone held the warmth of the sun.

John held the stone for a long time. Then his eyes met Jesus's. "The scorpion's sting is the truth of this world," he said. "It is deadly unless you suffer its pain until it leads you to another world. I will help you on the journey."

John handed the stone back to Jesus and watched as he slipped it under his tunic. Then the cousins walked together by the shore of the Salt Sea, leaving Judas forgotten and alone.

CHAPTER 20

Nazareth

One night Ozeret woke to the sound of the door slowly opening and felt a rush of cold, wet air. The door closed, and the room was filled with Jesus's presence.

Mary pulled open her bedroom curtain and rushed to her son. She embraced him and then pulled away to look at him in the light of the oil lamp Ozeret held.

Jesus stood smiling down at his mother, water dripping from his cloak and hair. He went to the door to get his mother's blue mantle and wrapped it around her as she stood shivering on the cold stones.

Ozeret set the lamp on the table and was startled by the lines on Mary's face and the white streaks in her hair. Mary looked like an old woman standing next to her son who had grown even taller in the months he had been gone. He now had a full growth of beard.

Jesus seated his mother at the table. Then he stirred up the fire and added two large pieces of sheep dung from the stack of fuel in the corner.

By this time Mary had regained her composure and commanded in her usual voice, "Hang your cloak by the door, Son, and then fetch dry clothes from your chamber."

Jesus did as his mother asked. Then he sat quietly while Ozeret, her hands trembling with joy, bathed his feet and trimmed his beard and hair. He was silent during the meal Ozeret set before him. After his supper he bowed to his mother and nodded to Ozeret. Then he entered the privacy of his bed chamber.

He couldn't sleep. The bed felt too high and too soft and the linens too smooth against his skin. His mind was foggy from the wine he had drunk, and his belly felt heavy from Ozeret's rich stew. He felt his ribs and his jutting hipbones and his belly swollen from an unaccustomed meal.

He missed the hard ground under him and the simple food he foraged for and ate while he stayed with John. He tossed restlessly on the unfamiliar comfort of the bed and listened to Ozeret clear the table and wash the dishes. He got up and watched through a slit in the curtain as Ozeret opened the spice cabinet. The scents conjured up Egypt and the caravans that passed through Mataria and the markets in Jerusalem crowded with people from the whole diaspora of his people and the meals Ozeret prepared, silently and with subtle skill, day after day throughout his childhood.

Ozeret turned. He felt her eyes find him behind the curtain, in the darkness. Then Jesus knew what he had missed during the winter in the caves, what caused him to get up early one morning before the sun had risen and roll up his blanket and leave without a word to Judas or his cousin.

It was her love he missed. The love that he tasted in Ozeret's lentil stew. The love he felt when she bathed his feet.

Finally Jesus felt tired enough for sleep. He went to Ozeret and stood before her and said, "I thank you, Ozeret."

Then he went back to his room and slept a long and dreamless sleep.

CHAPTER 21

Nazareth, two years later

Mary seemed content. The Magi's gold, a gift to her son so many years ago, was now funding her son's education at the Temple.

Ozeret felt the desperation in the young man when he came home from Jerusalem for a brief visit after Passover. It was full spring in Galilee. Seas of brilliant anemones danced among the fragrant herbs that perfumed the air. Jesus was up at first dawn and spent every moment of daylight in the hills. Each evening when he entered Mary's house, his face ruddy from the sun and with the fragrance of new life clinging to his tunic, Ozeret bathed his dusty feet before she served the evening meal. She rejoiced to see him becoming himself again, emerging from the pallid, somber young man who had entered the village a few days before.

Each night, as Ozeret scraped the leftovers into her own cracked bowl and scrubbed the plates and goblets, Jesus argued with his mother. Why must he return to the Temple with its dead rules and rituals and endless bloody sacrifices? The Sadducees said there was no life after death. How could that be true? Where was Joseph now? Was such goodness lost forever? Why couldn't he stay in Nazareth and try to live a simple, good life like Joseph?

Ozeret caught herself holding her breath, willing Mary to free Jesus from bondage to the god of the Temple. She remembered Anne arguing with Joachim, railing against the god of death and hopelessness. Jesus shared Anne's spirit. Why must Mary be like Joachim?

But Mary was implacable. Ozeret heard her calmly insist, "You must learn our god's words and laws. You cannot free our people from bondage until you become one with the Word and understand the chains that bind our people. And so you must return until your studies are complete and your wisdom far exceeds the knowledge and understanding of the scribes and Pharisees and Sadducees."

Jesus yielded to his mother's will, as Joseph had before him. But Ozeret felt his turmoil and ached for the squandering of his youth and vitality inside the lifeless Temple walls.

After he left Ozeret's ears ached for a voice to speak her name, and her heart grew numb with loneliness. Day after endless day, after Jesus returned to the Temple, she moved through the rhythm of life in the village where she was no more noticed than a stray dog.

Mary took for granted the water jug being filled from the cistern in the courtyard or the village well, meals fragrant with herbs and spices appearing on her plate, her feet being washed and her hair being combed, the house swept and the furnishings polished, the linens cleaned and aired and smelling of lavender, a plentiful supply of thread ready for her loom, and a peaceful silence all about her.

Ozeret shrank and shriveled back into herself, feeling once again the desolation of the beggar girl she had once been. She shivered and hungered and thirsted for the warmth and food and drink that Mary's home could not provide.

When her chores were done and her mistress occupied with scrolls or her loom, Ozeret crept out of the house and wandered the hills beyond the village. Sometimes she spread her black cape on a bed of herbs and lay down, pressing the fragrance into the cloth so she could bring it home with her. She closed her eyes against the blue of the sky which reminded her of Mary's cape and seemed to exclude her from the peace of the hillside. She only liked the sky when it was overcast or blackened by night. Then she could look up and breathe.

Sometimes Ozeret saw a shepherd in the distance, but he never had the height and gait of Judas. She wondered where he was and missed the sound of his voice speaking her name. Was he still in the caves by the Salt Sea? Ozeret wondered if Mary ever thought about the father of her son as she sat weaving at her loom or studying her scrolls. And what of Jesus, old enough now to father a child himself. Did he ever think about Judas? Did he wonder who his father might be?

Maybe Judas was dead. Ozeret heard the villagers talk about the Zealots who risked their lives to fight against Roman oppression. The son of Mary's youngest cousin had run off to join the Zealots, and she often wept her fear for her son as she waited at the well with the other village women.

Ozeret also wept, but alone and in darkness while her mistress slept. She wept for Anne and Joachim and for Joseph and Judas and for Jesus far away in Jerusalem. And she wept for herself. And after she had cried until there were no more tears, she felt empty and clean, like a hillside of herbs fragrant and flattened from the pelting rain of a violent shower. Peace would enter her then, and she would sleep.

Mary sat at the table after Ozeret had cleared away her plate. She had a wooden slat before her and the purse of coins. The purse was almost flat now. Roman taxes and Temple tithes and tuition took a heavy toll, especially since Mary had no source of income except for her loom.

Everyone in the village was suffering. No one, not even her own family, had coins to spare for the reclusive widow who never shared her troubles or the sorrows of her neighbors.

Ozeret heard the village gossip about Mary, a widow with an able-bodied, unmarried son, sending Jesus to Jerusalem to receive an expensive education while she grew old alone. She heard the scorn in villagers' voices when they spoke of Mary's son, a bastard raised to be a carpenter, who was too good to help out in the village.

Ozeret felt her own isolation deepen and woke each night from a nightmare of falling into the darkness of an empty well.

But always her mistress remained calm and unperturbed. She ignored the disdain of her neighbors and moved each day from loom to scroll to meal to bed. And at night, behind the bedroom curtain, Mary spoke into the darkness, pausing to listen to the voice that still guided her but remained inaudible to Ozeret's straining ears.

Ozeret glanced over Mary's shoulder at the wooden slat Mary used when she counted coins. Columns of marks were incised in the wood. Most of the marks had been scratched out. Mary opened the purse and put the coins on the table. Ozeret counted them, a skill she had acquired from her first mistress who taught her how to prepare the thread on a loom for weaving.

Ozeret remembered that there had been nineteen shekels and one gold coin when Jesus first went to Jerusalem to study in the Temple.

Each year, the Roman tax collector came to the village to bully the farmers out of a share of their crops and the shepherds a portion of their flocks. Since Mary had neither, he demanded coins.

The Temple tithe collector levied a half shekel for Jesus, the male in the household. The Temple priests collected more coins for the young man's tuition and board.

Now all that remained on the table were ten shekels.

Ozeret watched in amazement as Mary put her head on the table, scattering the coins with a dissonant clatter, and cried harshly and hoarsely, her throat unaccustomed to the expression of sorrow.

As quickly as it had begun, Mary's grief was silenced. Mary straightened up in her chair, replaced the coins and the wooden slat in the purse, and went into her bedchamber. She didn't seem to notice Ozeret as she brushed by.

When Mary returned to the room, her face was wiped clean of tears and agitation. She went to the door and signaled to Ozeret to follow her.

They walked quickly through the dusty streets of the village. The air felt dry against Ozeret's face. It hadn't rained in many months, and the blue of the autumn sky looked as beautiful and unrelenting as the cloak on the ramrod straight back of her mistress. Mary stopped at an open door and bowed her greeting to a courtyard full of children. A girl of fourteen or fifteen nursed an infant while a stooped and wrinkled version of the girl set a pot of lentil stew on the floor and handed each child sitting around the pot a piece of bread to use as a scooper. A boy, the oldest of the children and with the peach fuzz of early manhood on his chin, spoke a blessing over the meal. Ozeret guessed that the husbands of the women must be tending the family's flock.

When the children were eating with the quiet concentration of extreme hunger and, Ozeret guessed, the memory of missed meals, the older woman finally looked at Mary. She went over to the door, not even inviting Mary across the threshold.

Ozeret felt a sharp stab of sorrow for her mistress. She who had been the beloved daughter of a Temple priest and an educated woman in King Herod's magnificent Jerusalem had followed the words she read and the voice she heeded into this life of exile and disgrace.

The thought struck Ozeret that Mary was, in truth, less capable of hearing than she imagined her servant to be. The only sounds Mary heard were the voices of dead prophets speaking from parchment made from the skin of dead animals and the voice that spoke inside her own head. She couldn't even heed the voice of her own son when he pleaded to be free of her obsession.

The old woman summoned her oldest son from his meal. He glanced longingly at the pot of stew but obeyed his mother's command. Ozeret heard her own stomach rumble in sympathy with the gangly boy who looked as if he were growing even as he stood respectfully before his mother. "My cousin needs to speak to you," the woman said.

Mary slipped a leather pouch over the boy's head. "Take this to Jerusalem, Abraham, to the Temple," she said. "Find someone who can take it to my son. Show him this coin," she pressed it into Abraham's hand, "and tell him it will be his reward. Then wait in the outer courtyard by the stalls of the sellers of doves until my son comes to you. Do not return home without Jesus."

The woman glared at Mary, her hatred so strong that Ozeret could smell it.

"And why should I allow my son, the strength of the family while my husband and son-in-law are gone, to fetch your great rabbi of a son from Jerusalem?" she spat angrily at Mary.

Mary's face remained serene although Ozeret saw her recoil as her cousin's spittle sprayed over her.

Mary reached into the folds of her cape and pulled out a shekel.

"Cousin, this will pay the Temple tithe for your two men this year."

The woman's eyes grew wide, and she reached out a dirty, calloused palm to accept the coin. Then she bowed to Mary and rejoined her family in the courtyard.

Mary nodded to Abraham and led him to the outskirts of the village where she pressed another coin into his hand. "Use this to break your fast after your journey while you wait for my son," she ordered. "And buy food for the trip back home."

Ozeret watched the boy walk slowly up the path. She knew he had never gone to Jerusalem without a throng of family and villagers around him, and she worried about his first solitude and his arrival, alone, in the great city. But then she shrugged off her worry in the joy of Jesus's return.

CHAPTER 22

Jerusalem

Jesus bent over the scroll straining to read the lines he was to memorize that day. The light in the room was dim and the air was stale. Jesus's eyes ached and his spirit recoiled from the air and the drab uniformity of the young men around him. He stared off into space and daydreamed himself back into the vibrant hills of Galilee alive with spring wildflowers and the pungent aroma of herbs sweetened by spring breezes. Jesus resented his mother's plan to form him into a great priest and prophet. His years at the Temple had taught him that the Pharisees and Sadducees were killing the living god with their rules and rituals and blood sacrifices. He wanted to go out into the world and deep within himself to seek the truth.

As Jesus forced himself to focus once again on the long list of names on the scroll, he noticed, in the corner of his eye, a boy enter the room. The boy had a furtive air as he crept along the wall towards the corner where Jesus sat, and Jesus didn't recognize him as one of the students at the school. If one of the priests caught him, he would be flogged. Jesus wondered why he would take such a risk.

The boy slid a piece of parchment onto the scroll Jesus was studying and then slipped out of the room. Jesus recognized his mother's writing and, after reading the brief message, rose quickly.

Jesus hurried through the Temple complex until he arrived at the courtyard where his rabbi could customarily be found at that hour. He bowed his respect and waited for the man, not yet forty but with a face drained of color and vigor, to acknowledge him.

The rabbi looked up at Jesus, his brow under its black headdress creased with irritation. "You are to be studying," he said coldly.

Jesus bowed his acknowledgement. "I can no longer study with you," he answered. "My mother sent word that there is no more money for my education."

The rabbi looked startled but quickly composed himself. "You have a gift for understanding the Word and have almost completed your studies. It is expected that you will be a great teacher in a few years."

"My mother does not have enough money for the next payment. The tax collector exacted an unexpected fee this year. And the Temple tithe is due. I can no longer pay for your teaching."

The priest was silent for a moment. Then he said, "Gather your things while the sleeping quarters are empty and be on your way." And then he added, "Shalom. You have a gift. Use it well."

Jesus bowed and quickly left the courtyard. He had to cough to keep from laughing in joy and triumph. He hurried to the room where pallets were crowded together; each man's change of linens and cape hung on a peg over his cramped space on the floor. Jesus rolled his clothes inside his blanket and hurried to the courtyard where the money changers plied their trade.

Abraham was sitting in a corner of the courtyard. He stood up when he saw his cousin. Jesus pitied his look of relief. It must have been a frightening task to travel alone to Jerusalem and enter the Temple. He was amazed that his mother had been able to exact such a sacrifice. Then Jesus shook his head and smiled. His mother was a formidable force. She had controlled Joseph and she had dictated his own life. Why should he be surprised that she could exact such a journey from Abraham? Still, it was no small thing to get Abraham to leave his mother when the men of the family were away in the pastures. Perhaps Abraham would describe what had happened on their journey home. Jesus longed for talk of mundane matters almost as much as he craved solitude and the beauty of the hills.

Jesus embraced Abraham and kept an arm across his shoulders as they walked out of the Temple complex and hurried to the gate that would set them on the path home. Jesus could feel how thin his cousin was. He realized with a pang of concern that the taxes must have cut heavily into the family's crops and herd this year. He asked Abraham when he had last eaten.

Abraham hung his head and confessed that he had finished the food his mother gave him the day before. Then he reached into his tunic and pulled out a coin. "Your mother gave me this for food," he said.

Jesus stopped and looked at Abraham. "Why did you not buy food when you arrived?" he asked.

Abraham looked up and smiled. "What of you?" he asked.

They bought some food at the market far from the Temple where the poor of Jerusalem purchased what was necessary to survive and ate their meal leaning against a wall of a house near the square. When they packed what was left for the journey home, Abraham said, "It would seem we ate nothing of what we bought. Why does so much remain?"

Jesus shrugged his own bafflement. It was true.

Abraham was silent as they walked towards the gate. When they had left the city and were deep into the hills, dusty and dry under the harsh summer sun, he turned to Jesus and asked, "Why do we have so much food?"

Jesus was silent as they walked, thinking deeply about Abraham's question. His mind was used to memorizing rules and lists and rituals. It was crammed full of what to eat and how to prepare food and how to wash and the importance of cleanliness and purity and guarding the body from defilement. It took him a mile or more of walking and thinking to emerge from the mindset of the priests and enter the mind of his cousin. And when he did, he felt the world grow large and lush and simple.

"Abraham," he answered, as if his cousin's question weren't far behind them, "do you remember the flowers that bloom each spring?"

Abraham looked up and nodded at Jesus.

"Do we have to pay to make them bloom or toil to make them multiply?"

Abraham shook his head looking bewildered.

"That's the answer," Jesus said.

Abraham stopped in his tracks and stared at Jesus.

Jesus laughed and then, remembering the release of it, laughed some more.

"You didn't worry about your next meal or whether you had enough money. Your generous spirit trusted that sharing with me was all that mattered. And so we have plenty."

Abraham shook his head and walked more quickly. Jesus laughed again. He was so glad to be out in the world and in his own head and heart that he didn't care, for now, whether anyone else could share what he knew was true.

In another mile or two Jesus said, "Abraham, the Temple is so full of voices reading and reciting and the shouts of vendors and clinking of coins that a man cannot hear his own thoughts."

Abraham slowed down and answered, in a voice so low Jesus could barely make it out, "Hunger and cold and the crying of my brothers and sisters are all my mind can think of. So I keep it as blank as a rock seared by the sun."

They continued to walk in silence as clouds darkened the sky and the air began to cool. Suddenly the clouds opened and the first autumn rains began. They ran for a cave in the hillside and huddled in its shelter as the rain pelted noisily onto ground so parched it was as hard as the rocks and cliffs.

When the rain finally stopped, Jesus and Abraham left the cave and stood breathing the air washed clean of the dust and hellish heat of the long summer. They walked until the darkness, with no moon or stars, made them fearful of losing their way. Then they slept in a cave by the path, lulled by the rain that began at midnight and continued until dawn.

The next morning the path under their sandals felt springy and soft. The ground had loosened enough to accept the rain, and a shimmer of green covered the hills. Jesus laughed his joy. "Abraham, he said, "Thank you for setting me free."

Abraham took a sip of water and handed the goatskin to Jesus. "Cousin, I am glad for this journey," he replied.

CHAPTER 23

Nazareth

Jesus had grown taller and was very thin. He bowed to his mother and embraced her when she rose. Ozeret felt her heart expand with joy. The boy had truly become a man in the three years since his last visit, and his dark eyes looked wise and kind.

Jesus bent down to where Ozeret sat on her pallet with the thread she had been spinning dropped heedlessly on the floor. He helped her rise and addressed her with great courtesy.

"Ozeret, Abraham and I have been eating well on our journey, and we broke our fast with some milk from a generous goat at daybreak. But now that we smell your most excellent lentil stew, we beg you to consider the midday meal."

Ozeret heard her mistress rebuke Jesus. "My son, have you forgotten that our poor servant is as deaf as she is dumb?"

Jesus replied, "She has ears to hear a voice which speaks to her with love."

Ozeret felt Mary's eyes appraising her and hung her head in confusion under the scrutiny. Then she felt her spirit expand, for the first time in her life, to fully occupy her space in the room. She was surprised by the strength she felt flowing through her. She went to the door for the water jug and signaled to Jesus to sit on the stool

Joseph had carved so many years before. Jesus smiled at her and pulled the basin from under the stool. He sat down and removed his sandals while Ozeret filled the basin. Then Ozeret bathed the feet she had washed and watched since she first counted their ten toes in Bethlehem. She felt Jesus relax and heard his sigh of pleasure as her hands massaged each instep and gently pulled each toe. Then she took each foot into her lap and dried it tenderly with a linen towel.

Jesus fastened his sandals while Ozeret took the bowl of water to the street and emptied it into the gutter. After she refilled the basin, he took it from her hands.

"Abraham," he said to his cousin, "allow me to wash the dust of our journey from your feet."

Shocked silence filled the room. Then Mary spoke. "Son, our servant will perform that task while I prepare your meal."

Jesus turned to his mother and said, in a voice of authority, "My cousin has served me well in bringing me out of the Temple. Now I shall be his grateful servant in my home."

Then he beckoned to the nervous boy who stood glancing fearfully at Mary. Abraham reluctantly seated himself at the stool as Jesus commanded.

Ozeret heard a humming sound begin inside her head. Without waiting for her mistress's permission, she opened the spice cabinet and chose a prodigious assortment of seasonings—cumin, cinnamon, ginger, salt, pepper—to stir into the pot of lentils. As she stirred the pot, the room filled with a complexity of fragrance and Ozeret had a sudden memory, so vivid it jolted her and she almost spilled the stew, of the moment in Bethlehem when the astrologers visited Mary and presented her baby with their gifts of gold, frankincense, and myrrh. That long-ago room had been transformed by odors so wonderful that the air hummed with promise. Just like now.

Jesus finished drying Abraham's feet and emptied the basin once again. Then he led his cousin to his own chair at the table and sat himself where Joseph's seat had long been empty. "Ozeret, fetch your master's plate for my cousin's bread," he commanded.

Ozeret felt Mary's outrage quiver in the air and couldn't move. She looked at the shelf where Joseph's plate leaned. It gleamed from the oil she rubbed into it each day as she remembered the kind and patient man who had used it while he lived.

Jesus stood up from his seat, Joseph's seat, at the head of the table, and walked over to the shelf. He lifted the plate from the shelf and carried it to Abraham and said, "Eat from the plate of a good man, a true son of David, and be blessed."

Then he sat again in Joseph's chair, bowed to his mother, and reached to dip his bread into the aromatic stew.

Time dragged for Jesus. When he left the house to escape his mother's sorrowful gaze, Jesus heard the villagers whisper, just loudly enough so he could hear them, that all his expensive schooling hadn't taught him to be a carpenter like Joseph.

One day a stone grazed his ear as he was walking home from an afternoon in the hills. He barely glimpsed a couple of village boys as they ducked around the corner of the village synagogue.

Jesus despaired at his own uselessness. He had nothing to contribute to the modest economy of his mother's household. He was just one more mouth for Ozeret to feed. The village rabbi despised him as an upstart. Even his mother seemed to have given up on him.

By the time full spring brightened the hills and perfumed the air, Jesus was on his way. Only Ozeret and Abraham were sorry to see him go.

CHAPTER 24

Jordan River

Jesus travelled again towards Jerusalem and then on the narrow track towards the Jordan River. He followed the pilgrims who flocked to his cousin to be baptized in the Jordan, away from the Temple and priests.

His cousin looked gaunt and wild. His long hair was matted into thick locks, and his fingernails had grown so long that they were beginning to curl inward. His bare feet were filthy, and his camel skin reeked of sweat. John's eyes were hollow and smudges of sleeplessness darkened the skin below them. When he spoke or ate, Jesus saw that his teeth were black and pitted. There were already two gaps where teeth had fallen out. And his breath was like the stench of a rotting carcass.

And yet there was kindness in his brown eyes with their flecks of gold. And the words he spoke, warnings of the end times soon to come and the need for repentance, were warmed by compassion.

Many said John was the messiah. People flocked to John whenever he went to the Jordan River. Jesus saw the effort it caused his cousin to leave the solitude he craved, a stillness that hummed with the presence of his god. Yet he tried to bring others to his understanding of the goodness beyond this fallen world and hidden in each human heart. Jesus was in awe of his cousin, both for his beliefs and for his willingness to help others. He often stood in the midst of the crowd watching John baptize sinners and turn them into people of hope. And, with the whispering crowd, he often wondered if his cousin was the messiah the people of Israel had long awaited.

At first Jesus tried to talk with John. He told him about the sterile teachings of the priests and the cruelty of the Nazarenes. He asked John if he was the messiah and where he got the authority to preach and baptize. But John just listened and shook his head, refusing to answer Jesus's questions or talk about his own strange visions.

One night when autumn was far advanced and even this arid wilderness had felt the relief of rain, Jesus and John sat in the entrance to their cave enjoying the freshness of the night air and the brilliance of the moon. John broke the silence. "I am your messenger, Cousin," he said. "I prepare the way. But the gift of salvation for our people is within you and you alone."

Then John bent his head and wept.

Desolation swept over Jesus. He looked up and saw a cloud crossing the moon and darkening the hillside. And he knew with the uncomplicated grief of a child that John would die and he would die and life would go on. He felt nothing within him but darkness.

Jesus reached within his tunic and pulled out the scorpion. Pain ran through his palm and up his arm and settled in his heart. He thought of Judas and wondered where he was on this desperate night.

Jesus felt his cousin's arm on his shoulder and looked up. The cloud was scudding past the moon, and John's eyes gleamed from the tears he had shed. Jesus stood and embraced his cousin and with him all the filth and despair of the world. Then he walked down the hill and towards the Sea to spend the night with the darkness and the moon.

CHAPTER 25

Nazareth

Soon after Jesus left Nazareth, Abraham disappeared. His mother came to Mary's house and screamed at her cousin, but Mary sat without moving. Mary's cousin left empty handed. How could Mary give away the few precious coins that remained at the bottom of her trunk behind the bedroom curtain?

A few weeks later Abraham crept into Mary's house under cover of darkness. Abraham told Mary that he had found his way to the Jordan River. As he stood waiting his turn to be baptized, he felt a hand on his shoulder. Jesus was standing beside him.

***Ozeret could picture** the scene as clearly as she used to picture the stories Anne told Joachim behind the bedroom curtain. She saw the river, much broader than the torrents that swept down the hillside after a heavy rain and much calmer as it travelled across a flat plain. She heard the murmurs of the crowd of men waiting their turn by the river and felt the hairs on her arms rise against the cool breeze.*

Abraham had watched Jesus enter the river. As John poured water on his head and spoke the blessing, a great wind came up causing the trees by the river to sway and driving the clouds across the sky. The sun appeared and an eerie silence fell over the river. Then the wind calmed and the clouds returned and Jesus climbed out of the river to retrieve his clothes. His face looked strange, Abraham told Mary, and he quickly disappeared into the crowd.

Ozeret stared at Abraham feeling envious of his encounter with Jesus and wondering at his own changed appearance. Abraham stood tall and straight and confident with a strength that was more than the muscles that had recently filled out his body and turned him into a man. She was astonished to hear him tell Mary that he was leaving Nazareth to follow John. His mother had refused her blessing. He begged Mary for hers.

Through all this, Mary sat very still and her expression was, as always, inscrutable to Ozeret. Finally Abraham shifted his weight and cleared his throat and Mary fixed her attention on him. She spoke in a clear, firm voice. "Abraham, the one you must follow is my son, not his cousin. You must follow him and bring me news from time to time."

Mary went into her bedroom and returned carrying the purse which contained the last of her money. "Take this for your journey, Abraham," she said, "and see that my son has food to eat and clothes to wear. Now be on your way."

Still Abraham knelt before her. Mary looked at him impatiently.

"I beg your blessing, as the blessing of my family, on this departure from my village and my people," Abraham implored, sounding to Ozeret like a young boy once again.

Mary looked at him and smiled. Ozeret discovered that she had been holding her breath. She let it out and continued to watch.

"Shalom, Abraham," Mary said. "May the god of your namesake Abraham guide your journey and protect you and my son."

Abraham rose and was gone.

After he left, Mary took her face into her hands and wept, whether in joy or in sorrow, Ozeret could not tell.

CHAPTER 26

Jordan River

When Judas left the Salt Sea to follow John to the Jordan River, he felt the tail of the scorpion sting his heart with a new sense of purpose and clarity. He Judas, bastard and outcast, would help bring an end to the rule of the priests and King Herod and make way for the message of John.

Several times, on many different occasions, Judas joined the throng of penitents by the Jordan River and waited his turn to be saved. But each time he came close to the edge of the river, the scorpion around his neck would grow hot and his heart would be jolted into knowing, as he had always known, that he was doomed. He was part of the evil, damned world.

John preached the end of this world. Judas liked that message. This world had brought him nothing but misery and shame and the dark cloud that overshadowed his mind and left his hands bloody and his soul in turmoil. He looked forward to the end of this world. But until then he wanted revenge on the Temple priests who took the people's money and gave them no hope. The priests who controlled the Temple, the aristocratic Sadducees who said there was no life after this one and lived their lives of luxury and ease on the backs of the working poor, they were teaching the lies that suited them and stealing hope for a better world from the hearts of their people.

And Judas hated King Herod Antipas. Like his father before him, he was a Roman sycophant and a power monger over his own people. He might harm John for his growing influence over the people of Judea. His father had massacred baby boys for fear of a rival. What would this King Herod do to John?

CHAPTER 27

Jerusalem

And so Judas left the Jordan River and returned to Jerusalem.

When Judas rejoined the Zealots he had left many months before, he felt as if he were stepping into a stagnant stream. Nothing had changed. Judas heard the same talk of ambushes and martyrdom that he had listened to over the many years that he had fought with them against the Roman oppressors.

As the men talked, Judas imagined crosses, dozens of them, crowded outside the walls of Jerusalem and scattered on the outskirts of villages in Judea and Galilee. Sometimes when he looked at his fellow Zealots, he saw them already nailed to crosses, their faces contorted in the agony of waiting for the weight of their bodies to slowly push the air out of their lungs allowing them to die of suffocation and despair. Or he saw the men who had already died this horrible death. And their women whom they couldn't protect.

One night in particular still haunted him. Roman soldiers had swaggered through a Judean village extorting their portion of the harvest and livestock. The wife of one of Judas's men, barely pregnant with her first child, was raped while Judas and his men were ambushing the sentries. When Judas and the other Zealots returned to the village, they were greeted by women keening over the defiled body. The woman's husband went back to the garrison and butchered as many of the soldiers as he could before he was subdued and later crucified.

And then there was Aaron who had not yet reached his seventeenth year when he was captured during a raid on a Roman garrison near Bethlehem and crucified with three other Zealots. His brother Reuben's mind had never returned from the horror of that time. Now Reuben was mute and full of murderous rage.

Judas had come upon Reuben in an alley wringing the neck of a kitten. The expression on Reuben's face that day had forever haunted Judas's rare hours of sleep. Soon after Judas fled to the Salt Sea.

But now he had returned to be the militant arm of John's mission. Now his enemies were the priests and King Herod. They taught the people to worship the god of the Temple, the god of this evil world. Judas would do what he could to hasten their downfall and make way for the god of John, for his son's sake.

Sometimes Judas forgot his new purpose.

When the wind blew from the west, the stench of rotting corpses and the terror of slow death blew over the western wall of the city poisoning the crowded alleys of the poor and the spacious Temple courtyards alike and inflaming Judas against every reminder of Rome. On those days Judas wanted to spring on every Roman soldier he passed and kill him right there in the streets of Jerusalem.

But when the wind shifted, as it quickly did, Judas remembered his fury was now directed against the selfishness and deception of the priests and King Herod.

Each of the men in Judas's band of newly dedicated terrorists obtained a job that allowed him to infiltrate the world of the Temple and the Palace. One man was a stonemason by trade. His body and mind were as hard as the stones he used to expand the walls of the Temple complex and build opulent palaces for the priests and their families. He drank with the other workers and learned of the lavish building plans of Herod and the price in taxes on the poor. He helped build the system of running water and airy squares that made the Temple complex and housing compounds of the priests a healthy oasis in the filth and foulness of the rest of Jerusalem.

Another of Judas's men, a gardener in the sumptuous palace of Caiaphas, the chief priest of the Temple, listened carefully to gossip among the wives of the priests as they sipped their spiced wine and ate their sweetmeats, oblivious of the dirty man weeding the herbs that perfumed their rancorous words.

A third of Judas's men cleaned the closets that stank of the bladders and bowels of King Herod Antipas and his family. This man often waited, invisible as a chamber pot, for the closet's occupant to leave and took note of who visited the house and what new treasures, purchased with the tax money of the working poor, decorated the rooms of the palace.

Judas often eavesdropped on the mutterings of discontent in the market in Jerusalem and smiled his satisfaction. His band of Zealots was spreading rumors among the people, rumors that were only slight exaggerations of the excesses and extravagances of the Temple priests and King Herod.

IN THE TWENTY years that Judas had used Jerusalem as the base for his terrorism, he had come to know every house and alley as well as each merchant in the Temple and the markets, rich and poor, throughout the city. He could read the emotions of the people in the city as well as he used to read the skies above his uncle's flock.

One morning the people's anger and fear were strung as taut as when, twenty years before, rumors snaked through the city about the planned massacre of all the baby boys.

The people said that John the Baptiser was dead, beheaded by the king.

Some whispered that he was killed for criticizing King Herod Antipas, who had married his brother's wife in defiance of human decency and Jewish law.

Others said that the king killed him because John was growing too popular among the people and preaching against the evil powers of this world.

A group of women crying and wailing by a well where Judas often went to gather useful information keened for the loss of John and spoke of Jesus as his successor.

Judas spent a restless night worrying about all he had heard and waiting for news from his spies.

The next day Amos, Judas's man in Herod's sumptuous fortress at Masada by the Salt Sea, returned to Jerusalem to tell a grisly tale.

Amos, panting with thirst and almost fainting with hunger and horror, described an evening revel at Masada. Herod Antipas was celebrating his birthday, and the kitchen had prepared every manner of fish and beast and wines and sweets, with no consideration of Jewish dietary laws. Amos told Judas he might as well have been watching a Roman orgy if descriptions of the Roman excesses that made their way by soldiers and merchants were true.

After the feasting, as Herod and his court reclined around the room, the young girls of the court, free and servant alike, danced their sinuous and seductive dances. Herod was most pleased by the dance of Salome, the nubile daughter of his new wife. Before the entire court, Herod, in drunken and lascivious boastfulness, offered her whatever she might wish, up to half of his kingdom. Amos watched Salome go whisper with her mother. Then she announced what she desired.

Here Amos paused to eat some figs and goat cheese and drink a few sips of watered wine. Then Judas unbuckled Amos's sandals and fetched a basin of water to wash his feet, despite Amos's protestations.

"There is no servant to serve you here," Judas smiled looking around the small, dark room that served as his current home and headquarters in Jerusalem. "Rest for a few minutes and then tell me the rest of your news."

Amos sat quietly while Judas bathed and dried his swollen feet, and then he resumed his report.

Herod rushed from the banquet hall. Amos crept out of the hall and followed Herod to the closet where he heard the king retch violently. Because it was Amos's job to keep the closet clean, he spent several minutes removing the mess Herod had made and spreading fresh herbs on the floor of the tiny room to freshen it for the king's next visit.

By the time Amos returned to his hiding place in the banquet hall, a horrified hush had fallen over the room. Each man and woman and girl, except those so drunk they were slumped over without any awareness at all, sat in silent waiting.

Amos hid behind a curtain and waited too.

In time there was a bustle from the direction of the stairs that led to the dungeon where Herod held prisoners awaiting crucifixion. A servant appeared in the doorway carrying a serving platter. On the platter, lying in a pool of blood, was the head of John.

Judas reached out and placed his hand on Amos's arm. Both men sat in silence. To die as a party favor at a drunken banquet. Judas felt his gorge rise and the darkness overtook him.

When Judas came to himself, Amos was standing by his chair looking down anxiously at him. Judas tried to pull himself together for the young man, not much more than a boy, who awaited his orders.

"Amos," he said. "I do not want you to return to the fortress by the Salt Sea or to Herod's palace here in Jerusalem. Your absence today will have been noted, so you must disappear." Amos lowered his head as if he had been rebuked.

"You did right, Amos, in coming to me as you did, not waiting for Herod to return to Jerusalem. I needed the news you brought, and I needed it right away. Now here is your new assignment. Go find Jesus of Nazareth and guard him day and night."

After Amos left, Judas sat without moving for a long, long time. Then he put his face in his hands and wept.

Chapter 28

Galilee

What dismayed Judas, as he hurried along the path that led through Judea into Galilee, was that Jesus would now be the focus of Herod's paranoia. Not only that, Judas worried about the scribes and Pharisees and the Temple priests plotting against his son, now that John was dead. A prophet who preached against those in power was even more vulnerable than the Zealots. At least he and his men were armed and, when all went well, anonymous. John had been beheaded. What would become of Jesus?

And yet Judas felt proud of his son. He, like John, was showing people the evil of this world and giving them the hope that they might escape its futility.

Once men and women had spoken directly to their god. Now the priests and the Temple and a labyrinth of rituals and rules had supplanted the relationship between god and his people. People no longer trusted their own role in redeeming the world and each other.

Judas patted the purse under his tunic. It was almost empty. Each of his men contributed what he could from the job that was his base for spying on the priests and the Herodians. But Judas needed more operatives to assess the situation created by the murder of John.

Judas felt contempt for the bleating sheep who believed that a messiah with the correct religious and political lineage would lead the people out of bondage and give them power in this world. This world was evil. To be powerful in this world was evil. Still he must protect his son. And to do that he needed money and men.

An image of Mary, lovely in her sky blue robe, passed through his mind. She had pretended to love him and then, when he had planted life in her womb, she betrayed him and claimed Jesus as hers exclusively.

Fear loosened Judas's bowels. News of John's beheading would be travelling fast. Had it reached Nazareth? What would Mary do now that John, the chief rival to her son, was gone?

Judas walked quickly through the hills and by nightfall found himself far from Jerusalem. He had left with nothing but his purse and was desperately hungry and thirsty.

Judas saw a shepherd in the distance. He walked towards him.

The boy was very young and looked frightened when Judas approached him. Judas remembered his own loneliness and fear when Zachariah first sent him alone to watch the flock; his imagination filled the hills and skies with demons and darkening thoughts. But then he realized that the boy was afraid of him.

Judas wondered what he looked like. He was dirty and distraught and carried with him the corruption of violence and deception and the dark cloud that always hovered about his mind ready to fill him with rage and despair.

Judas attempted to compose himself and greeted the boy with the blessing he had learned from Elizabeth so many years ago. The boy returned the blessing and handed Judas the bowl he had been drinking from. He led Judas to a sheep who was bleating her desperate, monotonous misery.

"Her lamb is lost," the boy said. "I cannot find her lamb. She has an abundance of milk. Take it and drink."

Judas knelt down beside the sheep and filled the bowl with milk. He drank deeply and felt his strength return to him. When he was finished, he rose and smiled at the boy. "What news is in these parts?" he asked.

Words spilled from the boy. He told of a recent wedding in the next village, the village of Cana. His cousin had been married, and his uncle had nearly been disgraced when the guests consumed all the wine before the feasting was done. For guests had travelled from throughout the hills. His family was widespread. Many of the guests were people he had never before seen.

The boy went on and on in the rambling fashion of children who see everything of equal importance and weary the adult listener with the string of details and the absence of a point. Judas felt his gratitude for the supper of warm milk turning to exasperation and the wish to be shed of this tiresome child. But then a detail caught his attention.

"The man's mother was wearing a blue robe that my mother admired very much and she had with her the man called Jesus who is her son. My mother was glad when she heard that Jesus was coming to the feast. She allowed me to come too even though my father was very angry. And he was right. We lost a lamb while I was in the village.

After the wedding my father walked with me back to check the flock and when he discovered the lamb was missing, he beat me. I know my mother suffered too when he returned home."

The boy stopped his story to remember the beating. Judas stared at him in growing amazement. He wanted to question the child but had no idea what to ask.

The child's face changed from recalled misery to discovered gladness as swiftly as a cloud uncovers the sun on a windy day.

"The lost lamb gave each of us our supper tonight," he laughed. "This morning my father took away my pouch of food as punishment for losing the lamb, but he forgot that the lamb's mother would feed me."

"What of Jesus and his mother?" Judas asked desperately.

The boy grew serious. "My mother says Jesus is the messiah. For he controls the very nature of water."

Judas waited for the boy to continue and then shook him roughly. "Go on," he whispered.

The boy looked up in fear and spoke submissively and with a coherence that eased Judas's impatience.

"I was standing near the steward of the wine for the wedding feast. I heard the steward warn my uncle that the wine was all gone. Mary heard him too and whispered something to her son. I saw him shake his head. I do that too sometimes, and it makes my mother angry."

Judas shook the boy's shoulder again and he returned to the story. "Jesus's mother whispered to him again, and he stood up and walked over to the steward. He told the steward to fill the empty jugs with water from the cistern."

The boy looked his disgust, and Judas grimaced. The water in the cistern in the courtyard was for cooking and washing. No one would drink it. Was Mary mad? How could she suggest that it be offered in the place of wine at a wedding celebration? And how could Jesus go along with her suggestion?

The boy told Judas that he helped the steward fill the empty jugs and carry them back to the hall where the feasting continued. He watched the steward fill the bridegroom's goblet and waited for his contentment to turn into outrage. Instead, the bridegroom patted the steward's arm. When the host brought his refilled goblet to his lips, his eyes filled with amazement, and as the rest of the guests were served, a murmur of approval went around the room. The boy heard the guests whisper their amazement that their host had saved the best of his wine for last.

"What of Jesus and his mother," Judas asked the boy.

The boy looked uncomfortable for a moment and then he said, "I heard him rebuke his mother. He told her it was too soon. He said 'I am not ready' and then he bade his host farewell and left the feast."

Judas reached into his purse and handed the boy a coin.

The boy shook his head. "I cannot accept this," he said. "You have purchased nothing from me. What would my father think if I returned from the hills with money?"

Judas saw the fear in the boy's eyes. So he took the coin back. "You are right," he said. "This can bring you nothing but trouble. So take my thanks instead. And remember the story you told me this evening. Perhaps your mother is right. Perhaps you have seen the messiah."

Judas stood on the outskirts of the crowd. All day people streamed to this place where his son had retreated for a little peace. For hours they had sat scattered on the hillside, children playing quietly or napping by their parents, infants nursing at their mothers' breasts.

Judas made his way through the people. He saw how they attended the voice of Jesus; he felt the calm that prevailed. Judas remembered the anger in the crowds he had helped stir up in Jerusalem and Bethlehem and the other towns and villages of Judea. Anger and violence had turned speech into a bestial roar. Judas had seen small children trampled in the rebellious crowds and had felt the cloud that so often darkened his own heart engulf friend and foe alike.

But here in this wilderness, among a multitude much larger than any rebellious mob he had ever known, Judas felt peace shimmering just above the heads of the people and marveled that his son possessed such astonishing power.

Judas worried that these people would soon notice their hunger and thirst. The noon hour was long past, and words could not satisfy their appetites forever. Even now some of the children were starting to whine and tug at their mothers' skirts.

Judas drew close to Jesus and whispered his concerns. "You must send the people away before they grow restless and unmanageable," he counseled. "I know the fickleness of crowds."

Jesus smiled a welcome to Judas. "I saw you from a distance," he said. "Your red hair and great height let me know that it was you. I wondered when you would come to me."

Jesus started to laugh. "The man you ordered to follow me and keep me safe is watching on the outskirts of this crowd. He has been my constant shadow. Even when I send my disciples away and seek refuge in the most remote of caves, your man stalks me."

Then Jesus grew serious. "Judas, your man cannot protect me from the fear within my heart. And that is the greatest danger of all."

Then the smile returned and Jesus put an arm around Judas. "I thank you for your care," he said.

Judas felt a great weariness overcome him. He sensed no darkness, just the feeling that he would like to sink down on the ground and wait for the peace of death. His son was a strong leader. His words were guiding people towards hope and a rejection of this world of cruelty and deception.

Judas was ready to follow his son's path and lay down his arms. He was ready to acknowledge the weariness throughout his body and trust his son to keep the demons of darkness at bay. He was ready to be an old man at the end of his journey.

But then he heard a little boy complaining of his hunger and noticed an old woman, her eyes fixed on Jesus, trembling as she stood. Judas felt the darkness seep under his skin and crawl through his thoughts. These people are hungry and thirsty. They must eat and drink. But what does this young man know of such things? He feeds on visions and sips dreams of what might be.

Judas heard his own voice raised in anger against his son. Quiet fell among the people close enough to hear his words.

"I have brought bread for my journey and dried fish. I am beholden to no man for what I eat and drink. But what of this mob?"

Jesus turned to Judas and placed his hands on the old man's shoulders. "Judas," he said. "You measure by the standards of the world of men. But here on this hillside among these people the world of the father of goodness and plenty will prevail. Will you share what you have with these people?"

Judas took out the bread and the fish from his bag and handed the food to his son. Then he turned and walked away.

When he came to the edge of the crowd, he turned back for a last look at his son. But he couldn't see him. So he walked to a cave and sat in its shade. He felt his failure as a physical weight pressing on his heart. And then he slept.

Judas woke to the laughter of children. Two boys were throwing bread pellets at each other while their father lazily reproved them. Judas walked out of the cave and looked around. Everywhere people were reclining on the ground eating bread and fish and talking quietly. Young children lay in their mothers' laps, their faces content in sleep.

Judas rubbed his eyes. He walked through the crowd until he saw his son sitting with three children. He heard the children giggle in response to some nonsense from Jesus.

When Jesus saw Judas, he stood up. Judas watched his son lay his hand on each child's head and smile their shared joke. Then he walked towards Judas. "The children have worked some magic," Jesus said. "The children and the food you shared."

Jesus started to laugh. Judas felt annoyance mixed with hunger.

"I told them to take your bread and fish and distribute them among the people. They thought it was such a good joke that they didn't even pause for a bite themselves. And when they offered your food to that group over there," Jesus pointed to fifteen or twenty people lounging on the hillside, "one of the women produced a loaf of bread she had been hiding for fear that her family would go hungry. Then another and another produced fish and passed it around and soon all were fed and knew each other."

Judas just stared at Jesus. He felt contempt for such a childish manner of feeding a crowd. A trick like this wouldn't work among his men. They were disciplined and knew the punishment that would befall them if they deprived their fellows of the provisions for a campaign.

He heard Jesus say, "You are tired and hungry and have fed a multitude with no attention to your own need. I have saved the best for you."

Jesus motioned Judas to sit on a rock and produced from the purse at his side bread and figs and fish and a goatskin of wine that was at first tart on Judas's tongue but sweetened as it went down his throat and moved through his body. Jesus waited until Judas had finished eating and drinking and then he said, with his eyes glistening, "I know who you are and thank you for being my father in this world.

He must have slept again. He woke to a gentle tap on his arm. A child was offering him a basket full of bread and fish. When he

ORPHAN HOLD
DO NOT SHIP

H1 – 000000000245

ISBN 9781939051837

CLIENT	Alternate Sourcing
STATION	TPP Receiving Station 03
HELD	2026 – 10 – 08 08:48

SHELF

If its order arrives, scan this label at a receiving station.

shook his head, the child's mother smiled at him and told the child, a girl of about five years, that all was well with the man and it was time to go home.

The shadows had deepened over the hillside while he slept and all around him people were gathering up their children and readying themselves to return to their homes.

Judas heard his stomach growl. The child giggled and then looked down, as if ashamed.

Judas took a piece of bread and a bit of fish from the child and nodded his thanks. Then he stood in the deepening gloom of the moonless night until the cold drove him to seek shelter in a cave where Jesus's disciples lay snoring. Judas wrapped his cape around him and lay in lonely wakefulness until, at first dawn, he saw Jesus creep into the cave and sleep. Then Judas too slept through the first hours of the new day.

Judas woke to an empty cave. He went outside and saw that the hillside was empty. All that remained of the multitudes from the day before were scraps of bread and fish that littered the ground. Carrion birds swooped down to carry off the rotting fish. Their cries filled Judas with desolation.

CHAPTER 29

Bethany

Ozeret helped Martha strip her brother's bed and followed her to the courtyard where they put Lazarus' linens in the cauldron to soak. The stench of death filled Ozeret's nostrils. She was exhausted from the long journey to Bethany. She longed to be back in Nazareth cooking in her own kitchen and sleeping on her own pallet. Martha was bossy and demanding. Ozeret never had a moment's peace in this house.

Inside women wailed. Ozeret's mistress sat with her hand covering the hand of Martha's sister Mary. Ozeret heard the young woman ask, over and over, "Why does he not come? Why does Jesus not come to join us in our grief? He heals strangers and Gentiles and lepers and unclean women. Why not Lazarus, our brother and his dearest friend?"

Ozeret studied her mistress's lined and haggard face. For four days Mary had sat in this house, with Lazarus' sisters, and suffered their disillusionment with her son.

Ozeret wondered what her mistress was thinking. She knew her own thoughts. She was sorely disappointed in Jesus. She could find no reason in her heart to excuse him for disregarding the illness and death of Lazarus.

And then the door opened and he appeared. He looked tired and dusty and distracted.

Martha rushed to him and berated him and tugged at the sleeve of his tunic. Jesus shook off her hand and sat down, heavily, in a chair at the table.

Ozeret hurried to the stove and filled a bowl with lentils. She placed the bowl before her master and held a goblet of wine to his mouth. Jesus drank and then nodded his thanks. Without eating he stood up and left the room. The women followed.

Jesus walked slowly down the dusty road that led to the outskirts of Bethany. Then he walked up the path to the cave where Lazarus' father and mother had been laid to rest three years before.

Jesus had grieved with Lazarus and Martha and Mary when their father and mother succumbed to a wasting illness. He had prayed with them as they anointed their parents' bodies and wept with them as he and Lazarus pulled the stone across the cave.

Where had Jesus been?

Ozeret could smell the fear that had settled somewhere deep within Jesus. She knew that its stench was too powerful for her herbs. She could feel the anger and disappointment and resentment that swirled around the little group standing in sullen silence before the heavy stone of the cave. Even her mistress was watching Jesus son with a furtive and suspicious look.

Ozeret stood at the edge of the grieving family and friends. She was glad to be an outcast. She wanted no part of these people.

A shadow fell over Ozeret. She looked up and saw Judas standing beside her, his face worried and his blue eyes dark with sorrow. He pulled the scorpion from his tunic and held it up for Ozeret to examine. He nodded in the direction of his son.

Judas whispered in Ozeret's ear. Then he was gone.

Soon her mistress and Lazarus's sisters turned to leave the tomb. Jesus stood alone, as unmoving as the stone.

Ozeret went up to Jesus. She stood on her tiptoes, knees creaking, and put her hand on his chest.

Jesus barely noticed her at first. Then he glanced down at the gnarled hand that pressed the scorpion beneath his tunic. Soon, so quietly that she could barely hear him, in a whisper that sounded like a prayer, Jesus said, "The sting of the scorpion has the power to kill and the power to save." Then he removed the stone from the entrance to the cave, as if it were no heavier than the curtain of his bedroom in Nazareth, and entered the darkness.

LAZARUS SAT AT the table, bathed and fed, but the haunted look remained in his eyes.

Ozeret waited impatiently for her mistress to be done with the meal and leave this silent, stricken house. She desperately needed to be back in Nazareth with her spice cabinet and fig tree and the solitude of her pallet in the night. She was frightened by what Jesus had done in bringing Lazarus back from death. She wondered about her own complicity with Judas.

The air in the room still smelled of death and abandonment. But the odor seemed to come from Jesus, not Lazarus.

No one spoke. Everyone avoided each others' eyes.

Finally Mary stood up. Chairs scraped across stone. Silently Jesus followed his mother out of the room. Ozeret paused in the doorway. Lazarus and his sisters were standing with downcast eyes. Ozeret turned and followed her mistress and Jesus.

CHAPTER 30

Nazareth

Ozeret stared into the cistern. She was frightened by her own reflection.

She must accompany Mary to Jerusalem for Passover. She didn't want to leave the house in Nazareth. Her spirit was still somewhere on the road from Bethany. Ozeret feared it would never find her if she left her home again.

Ozeret wondered about Lazarus. She wondered if his spirit had found its way back to his body. What if Jesus had raised his body from the dead, but his spirit had travelled elsewhere. What would it be like for Lazarus, a man no older than Jesus, to have to travel through the rest of his years in a body that was no more than skin and bones and blood without memories or thoughts?

Ozeret wondered about Jesus. What had he done to bring his friend back to life? What remorse did he feel for all the suffering he caused by staying away and then doing something so unnatural and shocking?

Ozeret would never forget the stench of Lazarus's dead body. No matter how many times she opened the spice cabinet door, that smell of flesh devoid of spirit filled her nostrils. And when she lay on her pallet at night and stroked her hair, her own flesh smelled of decay and despair. She had no hope. Maybe that's what spirit was. Hope. Maybe that's what she had left behind.

A shadow blocked the light reflected in the cistern's surface, and then she saw the face of Judas next to her own reflection. She felt his arm on her shoulder and watched his mouth move to say, "Shalom."

Ozeret looked up. Then she looked around the courtyard. No one else was there.

"I go to Jerusalem," Judas said quietly. "My son needs me."

Ozeret shook her head in confusion.

"He raised Lazarus, Ozeret. And Lazarus was truly dead for four long days. My son has the power to raise himself and confound the evil of this world."

Ozeret stared in horror at Judas. She thought of Lazarus and his haunted eyes.

"Jesus will enter Jerusalem in triumph," Judas went on. "His followers will greet him as their savior. Rome and Herod and the priests and scribes will fear his power and try to destroy him.

I will lead his enemies to him, Ozeret. But you must not fear them. They have no power over him. Their sting is of the scorpion, deadly on earth. But my son is the king of another realm.

I dare not tell his mother. But you must guard her and help her, Ozeret, and then, when it is over, she will be glad."

Then Judas was gone.

CHAPTER 31

Jerusalem

The garden danced with torchlight, just as it would dance with fireflies when summer heat had ripened the olives and harvest time was near.

Small groups of men and women formed and dispersed, talking quietly, the women weeping. From time to time, one person or two or three would gather around Jesus where he sat on a flat rock staring down at Jerusalem.

Jesus's bent figure seemed to implore silence. As the darkness deepened, hopelessness filled the quiet shadows and, gradually, one by one or in small groups, the people who had celebrated Passover with Jesus drifted away into the cliffs or under the sheltering rocks throughout the garden and up the Mount of Olives, extinguishing their torches as they settled down for the night. There they whispered and wept until sleep overcame them.

Ozeret watched through the night. Her body ached from the dampness of the hard ground. She looked at Mary from time to time and wondered at her ability to rest after what they had heard from her son that night at supper.

Ozeret could make out the figure of Jesus as he sat alone on the rock waiting for his death. She wanted to comfort him and to hear him speak her name. But this night was beyond human help.

Once Ozeret sensed the spirit she had lost on the road from Bethany after Jesus raised Lazarus from the dead. It was hovering in the dark outside the cave where she, a woman of six decades or more, sat hunched inside her black cloak shivering with despair. Ozeret wondered if she were dying. Was her spirit waiting for her to die?

A procession of torches approached from the city, and the olive trees glistened in rain that had been falling for an hour or more. Ozeret stood up slowly and then, forgetting her stiffness and the pain in every joint, ran down the hill to the rock where Jesus sat watching the approaching lights. She stood beside the rock and waited with him until she could make out the faces of the men led by Judas: clean-shaven Roman soldiers, Sadducees and Pharisees in their flowing beards and, on the fringes, boys and men from the city and beyond, their eyes hard with anticipation of the cruel sport to come.

A soldier shoved Ozeret out of the way, and the mob surrounded Jesus. Ozeret heard the hiss of rain extinguishing the torches and then all was darkness. She smelled fear in the mob and heard the men shuffling around in the dark like a flock of bewildered sheep. Then someone issued a command in the language of the Roman oppressor and the sound of marching feet receded down the path.

Wailing filled the darkness, streaming from caves and rocks and seeming to swirl around the trees in the garden. Then the men and women who had come to the Garden with Jesus grew silent again. They straggled back towards Jerusalem seeking, Ozeret supposed, the creature comforts of dry clothes and warm fires and the oblivion of sleep.

Ozeret stood on the rock where Jesus had waited and felt the clamminess of her clothes enter the marrow of her bones. She wished for death before the day that was to come.

Then she heard it.

At first she thought it was the keening of another woman who had stayed behind in the Garden. But then she realized that the sound was not a woman's grief.

As Ozeret hurried towards the sound, she began to make out the words coming from the bottom of the Garden, near the road to Jerusalem. "My son, my beloved son."

Olive trees dripped rain on her head as she hurried towards the familiar voice. Then all was silence.

An enormous, misshapen olive tree loomed through the misty air. Ozeret stopped and waited, summoning courage. As she drew closer, she saw that its massive trunk hugged the ground and was as knobby as her own arthritic hands and feet. She wondered if this tree, so much older than she was, ached in the cold of this cruel spring morning.

The rain began again, but gently, and Ozeret thought about the Passover supper just a few hours earlier. Her feet still felt the comfort of Jesus's touch. He had washed each person's feet—men, women, and servants. Many had protested, but only Judas had his refusal accepted by Jesus.

Before Judas left the room, he embraced Jesus. Ozeret, standing very near, heard Jesus whisper, "Forgive them, Father. Let me die. We must suffer the scorpion's sting."

The rain grew heavier and still Ozeret stood on the path, refusing to see what she knew was there. The creaking of an overburdened limb was muffled by the rain, but the stench of agony and fear poisoned the Garden.

Ozeret heard a step above her on the path and turned to see Mary, her blue cape sodden and her face bleak and tired, walking towards her. Mary stood by Ozeret and, shivering, moved closer.

And then, as if from a silent signal, they walked to the other side of the tree.

Judas stared sightlessly at them, the whites of his eyes gleaming in the damp gray of early dawn. Ozeret walked over to him and reached up for the short dagger at his side. Then she stood on the piece of wood Judas had kicked from beneath his feet and pulled herself into the tree. She crawled slowly and painfully towards Judas. The tree was slippery from the rain, and she almost fell. Mary pushed her until she regained her balance. She steadied herself against the pain in her shoulders and her hips and her knees.

The dagger was as sharp as the knife Ozeret used to chop vegetables for her stews. It cut quickly through the rope. Judas fell to the ground with a muffled thud.

Ozeret closed herself off from the pain she felt and the sound of Mary's cry. Then she inched her way back down to the ground.

The rain let up, and the sky began to brighten. Ozeret knelt beside Judas and closed his eyes. She examined him carefully and took what might be of use. Then she stood up and started down the path.

Ozeret thought about dry clothes and a meal for her mistress and for herself. She was tired of the sound of Mary's crying.

Mary tripped and fell heavily against Ozeret. Ozeret put an arm around her.

Judas's purse in her hand felt heavy. Ozeret realized she was crying. She wondered why. Then she understood. Judas was gone. The folly of what he had believed now claimed him and would soon claim his son.

Ozeret stopped. Mary turned to look at her. Ozeret saw in Mary's eyes the willful young girl who used Judas to conceive a child and Joseph to raise him. Then she saw in Mary the dispirited eyes of Lazarus and the horror in the eyes of Judas before she closed them just moments before.

Ozeret stopped crying. She felt her own spirit fill her like an indignant rush of air. Relief and certainty so strong that they felt like joy filled Ozeret. She moved quickly down the road, half dragging Mary beside her.

OZERET STIRRED THE stew and ladled it into her mistress's bowl. She watched the color return to Mary's pale face and light brighten her deadened eyes. Ozeret looked around the room to make sure they were alone.

Ozeret placed the purse on the table next to Mary's bowl.

Mary stared. Finally she looked up at Ozeret. "What is this?" she asked in a cold voice.

Ozeret heard her own voice answer, "It is a gift from your son's father."

At first Mary sat quietly as if she heard no more than a breeze stirring through the doorway. Then she looked up at Ozeret and said, "You speak."

Ozeret nodded. "If you have ears to hear, then listen."
And Ozeret told Mary what they must do.

THE SUN WAS directly overhead and hot for early spring. Ozeret tugged on the sleeve of the soldier and handed him a dripping sponge. "Offer this to my master," she said, "and his mother will reward you."

The soldier looked from Ozeret to Mary and smiled when he saw the silver that gleamed in Mary's palm.

Time seemed to move back and forth making Ozeret feel queasy. She looked up at Jesus and saw instead a baby shrouded in burial linen and shivering in dirty straw. Then the baby laughed and two small boys were eating lentil stew. They ran out the door and stood in a river. John's severed head bobbed in the current while Jesus watched from the branch of a tree.

Time lurched again, and Ozeret looked up at Jesus. He was nailed to the cross. She could smell his fear.

The soldier lifted Ozeret's rag up to Jesus on the tip of his sword. Jesus put his parched lips to the rag and grimaced at the bitterness of the infusion Ozeret had prepared in her own cracked earthenware bowl.

Twice more, as the sun moved across the sky and buzzards swooped and women wailed, the soldier dipped the rag in Ozeret's bowl. Twice more Jesus grimaced at its bitterness. Finally Ozeret watched his anguished face relax into death.

Then all was silence and darkness and the fading scent of herbs.

Afterword

There are few certain facts about the historical Jesus. We know the approximate dates of his birth (4 B.C.E.-6 C.E.) and his death by crucifixion (30-33).

I looked in vain for a historical record of Judas outside the gospels. We don't know when or where he was born or how he became involved with Jesus. What we have, in abundance, are stories.

The stories began as an oral tradition that, over time, was replaced by a written record. In the second century, while Christianity was increasingly beleaguered by Roman persecution, the diversity of stories became a liability. Christians needed to get their story straight. Iraneus, a Christian bishop in France, took a decisive step. Only four of the gospels—Matthew, Mark, Luke, and John—would tell the story of Jesus and Christianity.

Fast forward to 1945 when over 1000 pages of ancient documents, including lost gospels, were discovered near Nag Hammadi in Egypt. Many of these pages contain gnostic views, an outlook suppressed by official Christianity. Forget the resurrection of the body; the human body imprisons the divine spark of the true God of spirit. Enlightenment is the gateway to salvation.

In the *Gospel of Judas*, discovered later and made public in 2006, Judas is the only disciple who understands the gnostic story Jesus is telling. His alleged betrayal frees Jesus from a bodily prison.

Different stories.

Although Mary is mentioned just a few times in the canonical gospels, stories about her began in the second century and continue unabated to the present day. These stories inspired Medieval and Renaissance artists. Giotto's fourteenth century narrative cycle in the Arena Chapel in Padua, Italy includes visual stories about Joachim and Anne as well as Mary and Jesus. I found my imaginary Ozeret there, spinning thread and eavesdropping.

These stories have shaped Western culture, for better and worse, for close to two thousand years.

The Scorpion's Helper, a historical fantasy, grew out of my own relationship with these stories.

Some of the books and websites that were especially helpful in shaping my story include: *Giotto: The Arena Chapel Frescoes*, by Giusepe Basil; *Reading Judas: The Lost Gospel of Judas and the Shaping of Christianity*, by Elaine Pagels and Karen L. King; *Zealot: The Life and Times of Jesus of Nazareth*, by Resa Aslan; *The Gospel According to Jesus: A New Translation and Guide to His Essential Teachings for Believers and Unbelievers*, by Stephen Mitchell; *Alone of All Her Sex: The Myth and Cult of the Virgin Mary*, by Marina Warner; *Mary: A Flesh and Blood Biography of the Virgin Mother*, by Lesley Hazleton; *Signs and Symbols in Christian Art*, by George Ferguson; *Biblical Holy Places: an Illustrated Guide*, by Rivka Gonen; http://www.wga.hu/frames-e.html?/html/g/giotto/padova/index.html; http://ngm.nationalgeographic.com/ngm/gospel/; http://www.biblicalarchaeology.org/.

Acknowledgments

Michael Winship first imagined Judas as the father of Jesus. Eleanor Winship named Ozeret. Elizabeth Kostova reminded me that, whatever happens, writers write. John McMichaels listened and encouraged and advised for five long years.

Susan Sacher read my first draft. Her comments and enthusiasm kept me going. Deb Stanford, Alice Armstrong, Matt McMichaels, Marcia Chapman, and John McMichaels read early chapters and later drafts with insight and helpful suggestions. Joelle Fraser, my managing editor at Lucky Bat Books, polished the manuscript and guided me through the process of publication.

I'm grateful to them, to Cindie Geddes and Judith Harlan at Lucky Bat Books, and to all my family and friends who helped me find the voice to tell this story.

www.ingramcontent.com/pod-product-compliance
Lightning Source LLC
Chambersburg PA
CBHW061547250926
52052CB00010B/3102
* 9 7 8 1 9 3 9 0 5 1 8 3 7 *